GAME OVER

JA'NESE DIXON

PUBLISHING

Game Over.
Copyright © 2021 by Ja'Nese Dixon

ISBN-13: 978-1-950405-31-2 (paperback)

Printed in the United States of America.

Photo by Lindee Robinson Photography.

Model: Kwantais Meeks.

Design by Dana Pittman.

TABLE OF CONTENTS

SNEAK PEEK: PLAY TO WIN

Rules are meant to be broken. But can a secret romance between this pro football player and a single mother lead to love?

Emmitt Booker wears his playboy badge with pride. And thanks to his boys, he returns to Houston as head coach for a summer youth football camp. The moment his cleats touch the field, his attention isn't held by the awestruck boys but a very distracting curvy woman with amber eyes and cherry-red lips.

Amber Evans ignores the dolled up, whispering mothers, praying for a second of Emmitt's time. Men like him—smoky dark eyes, chiseled body, and filthy rich—make women forsake their god and their common sense for a taste.

She went down that road and knows where it ends: heartbreak.

Men like Emmitt don't settle for one woman when they can have two. Billionaires like him want nothing to do with real women, with real-world *ish* in their lives. She figures it's best to focus on one thing, the happiness of her son.

And when Kemen begs Amber to get him on Coach Emmitt's team, she'll do anything to make it happen. However, she doesn't expect Emmitt's illicit offer.

Fun and games turn to passion and lust as their desire builds into a blinding white heat, intense, all-consuming fire that sets their summer ablaze. On the field, he teaches her son to run, catch, and score. And in the bed, he teaches her to rush, tackle, and soar.

Emmitt aches for her. Amber longs for him, never forgetting that time isn't on their side. Her satisfaction is his goal. For the first time, he considers the possibility of his life being about more than his boys and football.

But could their little secret be more than a fling? Could *this* be love?

GAME OVER

CONTENTS

SNEAK PEEK: PLAY TO WIN

CHAPTER 1

I'M a unicorn with the magical ability to make a dollar out of fifteen cents. I can bend the minds of mere mortals, and I know how to bring men to their knees. *Most days.* Okay, this last one is sort of sketchy because lately I've only come across grown-ass boys. But I've digressed.

How? Well, that's the magical part. I'm a single mother with a thirteen-year-old son. I work in retail—hourly pay for standing on my feet and helping women squeeze in too small clothes. I shake my head because I too fell for jeggings, but they are not nice when you have thighs like mine. Thick thighs save lives, but in the wrong jeggings, they could start a fire.

I'm just saying…

Anyway, my magic isn't about spells or potions but timing. It's a gift passed from my grandmother to my mother and my mother gave it to me and I pray I'll never gift it to my son. Because this magic makes me daring, always prayerful, and some days, like today, it transforms to hope that it won't always be like this. And hope is a powerful thing.

"Now to stretch this dollar…"

I reach for the eraser, clearing off the master plan from last month, giving myself a fresh start. It was a doozy thanks to Kemen graduating from junior high. I thought I had at least four more years before I'd have to purchase a cap and gown. But my kid graduated at the top of his class and will enter high school a year early.

I feel the goofy grin spread across my face. I should get a #proudmamma tattoo on my forehead because my kid is crushing it on the field and in the classroom. Some days, I can't believe he's mine, but he is and I'm the crazy mamma hollering at every game, standing on every sideline because his success proves I'm not a fuckup. Not in this area of my life.

But with all the others—relationships, finances, career—I'm seconds from needing an intervention. I grab my basic spiral notebook with my figures and three different color dry erase markers. Pushing aside the inevitable for the immediate is how I survive from month to month.

Horizontal lines run the length of the board and vertical lines following. I scribble columns where I get paid. Every month, without fail, I'm at least five hundred dollars upside down. Hence my need for magic.

"Ma, where you at?"

"Back here, baby." I stand back with a hand on my hip.

"Here." He shoves the mail in my direction, kisses my forehead, and disappears.

"Wait, where are you going?" I juggle a little and start shifting through the mail. Windows with pink paper remain in the front, the junk mail gets tucked under my arm, and the last letter is from Jordan Preparatory Academy. "It's here!"

I walk down the hallway towards Kemen's bedroom. "Open it."

Kemen yanks a t-shirt over his head. His gaze darts between the envelop and me. Judging by his shirt and shorts, he's going out to play football. I step back, giving him room.

We applied to the prestigious private school in December. He had several interviews in March. Now, here we are in May.

These are the moments that leave me wondering where the time went. He's the reason I wake up and go hard until my head hits the pillow. But he's not my baby anymore.

I used to throw him on my hip, and over the last

year, he's morphed into a young man. His voice changed. He has a little peach fuzz on his chin. His hours in the gym and on the field have transformed my lanky son into a ripped athlete.

I exhale, suddenly unable to stand. The edge of his bed seems like the place to sit and wait. His walls are royal blue with posters of his favorite Dallas Cowboys. This is a big day for him... *Hell, for us.*

This six-foot genius is my world. I eat, sleep, and live to help Kemen reach his goals. It's just the two of us, and somewhere along the way, his dreams became my focus.

Mama's gotta have a life too, a voice whispers in my head and I push it aside. Not until my son enters college. He will graduate from high school. He will go to college. He will not be like me, working low-end jobs, surviving on magic and pure determination.

I want better for him.

Kemen walks over and sits beside me with the unopened letter.

"Dude, what's up with the long face? This is the next step."

"But none of my friends will be there."

"Kemen, don't do this. We've changed our entire lives to get you in this district to get into this school." A roll of agitation simmers in my blood.

"I know. I just...."

The tone of his voice captures my attention, and I wrap an arm around his shoulders. "You make friends everywhere you go. Brandon's right next door. You can see him after school. And you'll meet kids this summer at the engineering camp."

Graduating early and possibly transferring to a new school means he's starting over without his crew. Thankfully, my best friend Chanel and her son Brandon live next door. We're a cold-ass tag team juggling the boys together.

"Speaking of the camp…"

"Kemen, boy, you're going to make me drop-kick you in the throat." I groan, cradling my face in my hands. I literally just paid the damn camp off.

"Ma, you don't even reach my shoulders." He chuckles.

"Shut up." I look over at him staring at the unopened envelop. "What is going on here? What are you saying?"

"I know things are tight but…"

"But what?"

"I want to attend the football clinic at Knights Youth Sports Center. Brandon's going and they announced that Emmitt Booker's the head coach."

"And I'm supposed to know who this Emmitt guy is?"

"Yeah, Ma. He's the star running back for Dallas."

Kemen pulls out his cellphone and taps around. Then he holds it up to my face.

Well, hello Emmitt. A fine brotha with mahogany skin and a beautiful smile. But it's the spark of light in his eyes that makes my stomach flip-flop. His face looks familiar. I reach to get a better look and Kemen snatches it out of reach.

"Ma... stop smiling like that."

"Like what? That man is fine!" I lunge for the phone.

"Ma!"

"You can watch girls' asses and I can't tell you a man is good looking?" I roll my neck. "Am I not a woman?"

I've grown up with my son, and after my mother passed, he and I had to find a new version of our relationship. I have to be his mother, friend, and father since Nathan Russell, everybody calls him Nate, is unreliable.

"Yes, ma'am. You're a woman that has needs... yadda, yadda, yadda. But you still have four years." He reminds me of my vow to remain single until he graduates from high school. I dismiss him with a flick of my hand.

Kemen doesn't know all of my business, but he knows enough to give me space when needed. We're all human in this camp. I don't date because I don't have time for the games. Men, these days, will make you catch a case and I got shit to do. I have a few brothers I can call when I need business handled and I send them right back home.

"I'm waiting four more years, but a woman can, at least, window shop. Damn." I chuckle, reaching for the phone again. "Why does he look familiar?"

Kemen laughs and points at the poster on the wall.

"Oh, damn. That's because I see you every week when I'm searching for someone's dirty clothes." I talk to Emmitt, taking a dig at my messy child.

"You'd get with a ballplayer?"

"Nah. Not my type. But ain't nothing wrong with looking." I say the words, looking at Emmitt Booker on the flyer.

"You wouldn't know how to act with all those cameras in your face. You'd be elbowing chicks in the nose and acting a fool."

"And that's why I wouldn't date a ballplayer. I want a brother with a good job, benefits, and all his natural teeth." And who knows how to take care of *business* in the bedroom. But my son doesn't need to know that.

Kemen rocks back laughing. "What if he's nice? I'm sure he has a clean ride and a mansion. Wouldn't you like to live in a mansion?"

"I'm good." Experience has taught me that nice men are worse than players. They shower you with gifts and compliments. But most spit that same game everywhere they go. "We'll never know because I have four years to get you through high school and into college."

"He got a ten-million-dollar bonus last year. Can you imagine what we could do with ten million dollars?" Kemen sits up with stars in his eyes.

"Ten million dollars? I can only imagine the drama attached."

"Probably," he mumbles. "What kind of man would you date? For real."

I shrug. "I want someone I can come home to and just kick it. Money's cool but money doesn't solve all of your problems."

"Would you get married?"

"I'd like to. He'd have to love us both. He'd have to understand that you're my number one priority. He'd have to be a very special man."

I look back at the digital flyer. There's a sexy smirk on Emmitt's face, as if he doesn't have a care in the world. I could stare at him all day and not tire of those seductive eyes and juicy lips. But men like that are not on my radar.

I was born and raised in H-Town. Row houses, gold grills, and candy-coated whips. I don't want a street dude, but I want a man who can hold his own because I'm not a lightweight. I've been through hard times and I'm still standing, some days I'm stronger than others, and I have a lot of love to give. Too bad I wasted it on the wrong men.

I think about my ideal man often, but not through the lens of my youth. When it's time to date again, I want a brother to see me—all my layers, all of my flaws, and love me. I'm not checking cellphones or dirty drawers. I want a real man that knows where home is and lays his head next to me every night. Basically, I want forever, but until then, I'll raise my son and entertain gentlemen friends—when I can squeeze it in.

I pass the phone back. "What's this about? We have a rock-solid plan. You need more than football to get into an Ivy League school."

"Ma, I know. But this is a once in a lifetime opportunity. I really want to go to this clinic.?"

"What did your dad say?"

"Maybe next time."

"I'll talk with him." Nate and I agreed to split the cost for Kemen's expenses. Nate's still a football fanatic, so he covers Kemen's track and football expenses, and I pay for academics like the engineering camp. But Nate's world revolves around his trucking business.

"The clinic starts next week."

"I'll call him tonight." I promise, mentality calculating the last time I've talked to him. Nate and I have a complicated situationship. We've managed to co-parent, but his ass gets flaky when I cut off access to my cookie.

"Yes, ma'am." He doesn't sound convinced.

"Baby, I'm trying here."

"I know. Forget I mentioned it." Kemen gets up and tosses the unopened letter on his dresser. His defeated stance makes my heart ache.

"Don't you at least want to see if they accepted you?"

"You can open it." He slides on his gloves and grabs his football.

I walk over and pick up the letter holding my son's eyes. He doesn't ask for much. Maybe some gym shoes, a little cash to go to the movies. But he's fully aware of how my magic works. I'm stretching here and another camp just isn't in our budget.

"I'm good, Ma."

"How many times have I told you that lying to your mother is a sin against God?"

I get a *my mother is crazy* smile. "A million. Open it. The guys are waiting for me."

I nod, and with shaky hands, I tear open the envelop. The paper is thick and smooth. It feels fancy in my hands. We are moving into the big leagues. Then, my eyes focus on the first few words. Dear Mr. Russell and congratulations.

"You did it." I look at Kemen. "You did it, baby, you did it." I'm shouting, unable to control my energy. We've waited months for this letter. I spin around a little in a circle, not sure what to do next when I see him standing there like a statue. "What is wrong with you? This is what you wanted."

"No, Ma, it's what you want."

I'm at the intersection between elation and rage. "Kemen, you're freaking me out. Tell me what's going through your head before I lose my shit."

"Ma, I don't need to go to that school to go to college. I have a 4.0 GPA. I'm one of the best football players in the state. I *will* go to college. But I want to play ball."

My heart sinks.

My eyes glaze over as I hold the letter up. I have one child, and my life has been about loading all my eggs in this one basket. And his acceptance to the most prestigious private school in Houston makes me feel like I've done something right, for once. Like we win. And I'm not a fuckup.

However, Kemen doesn't get it and I'm sure it's because he's thirteen, but I was only a few years older than him when everything in my life changed. I can't let him make that same mistake. So, I have to help him see that this is what *we* want.

"Football isn't guaranteed. Kemen, do you know how many little Black boys dream of playing football or basketball? You have the intelligence to do anything you want. Son, with this you can write your own ticket." I hold up the acceptance letter.

"I don't give a damn about other kids. They ain't me." He stands ten feet taller.

"Watch your language."

"Ma, you taught me to believe in myself. I excel because I bust my ass, just like you. I study, I train, I don't eat junk food, I go to bed on time. I'll win because that's what *we* do."

God, I'm looking into my own eyes. I roll my head back and look at the ceiling.

"Mamma, do you think I like seeing you working for minimum wage, our car always on its last leg with no gas, shifting money around to pay the bills? This is our ticket." He holds up the football.

My mother would have flipped the fuck out if I gave her that same speech. She felt the same when I dropped out of high school to get my GED. But I refused to live on government assistance. Not if I had my right mind and an able body. She told me all the ways I was ruining my life. I won't do that to my son because I love him and I believe in him.

I know that if he wants this, I want it for him, even if I don't like it. This is when my unicorn status is cemented. Bending the minds of the unsuspecting can be a challenge, but it boils down to negotiating skills.

A win-win is always a win.

That means I need to get his ass in that football

clinic and make him a willing participant in the engineering camp *and* Jordan Preparatory Academy.

Win-win-win. I'm feeling like DJ Khaled.

And Kemen's going to Jordan Preparatory. I won't have my son banking on a pipe dream. I know he's good, but so are thousands of other kids. Kemen will *be* somebody, even if I have to drag his ass to the top.

"How about we make a deal?" I offer because everyone—even Kemen Russell—needs options. "I'll get you into that camp and you'll attend Jordan Prep with no bitching."

"Yeah, Ma. But how?"

"There's nothing I can't do. I'm a unicorn."

"The clinic costs a grand and it starts Monday. And Aunt Chanel said they don't have scholarships."

He's a chip off the old block. Had enough sense to ask about scholarships. I'll have to confirm with Chanel to make my plan work. I certainly don't have a grand sitting around, but I have a few tricks up my sleeves.

"When has that ever stopped me? Come on, youngin', quit stalling. I get you in and you'll start at Jordan Prep in the fall with a smile on your face." I extend my fist, holding his gaze.

"Bet." He pounds my fist and I exhale, relieved, but exchanging one issue for another. Kemen kisses the top of my head. "One day, I'll pay you back."

"You better."

"Love you, Ma." He heads for the living room and I'm on his heels.

"Be careful. And—"

"Look out for cars. I know, Ma, I know."

I watch until he disappears down the hallway. How do I get myself in these situations? I've just signed myself up to shuffle him across town daily. But first, I need to get my baby into that camp.

I don't stop until I'm in my bedroom. Calling Nate and Chanel are at the top of my list. Nate, for obvious reasons, Chanel because she works for Knights Youth Sports Center.

I text Kemen, *Send me the flyer. I need to call for the details.* My phone buzzes and I stare at the fine man on the flyer again. He is trouble with all capital letters.

I toss the acceptance letter and bills onto my dresser, weighing my options. The flyer gave general details, but I'll learn more if I call the center.

For the next thirty minutes, I'm passed from person to person until I'm transferred to the center director.

"This is Scarlette Knight."

I smile and put on my professional voice. "Good afternoon, Miss Knight. How are you?"

"Good. How can I help you?"

Well, damn. "My name is Amber Evans and I'm interested in enrolling my son in the football clinic."

"I believe we're at capacity. What's your son's name?"

I give Scarlette his first and last name, and after a few minutes, she discovers an application in the system.

"I don't see your signature. But you can sign it when you attend the orientation next Friday. Now to see if we have any seats left. Can you hold a minute?"

"Sure."

That boy of mine. He would submit the application and then tell me. I wag my head, waiting for Scarlette to return.

"Miss Evans, you're in luck. I have two seats left. To hold it, you'll need to submit the full payment of…"

She rattles off the clinic highlights, and my eyes buck. "Fifteen hundred dollars for a *youth* football clinic?"

"Yes."

"Do you offer scholarships or a sliding scale fee structure?" I ask.

"We had a limited number, and we have awarded them."

She rattles off the details and I'm running an interference in my head. How in the hell will I come up with fifteen hundred dollars in a week? I consider my options. Eight weeks is four pay periods. Quickly, I do the math and offer a solution. "Can I pay four hundred and the rest every two weeks?"

Four hundred dollars is a huge chunk of my check. But I'll have to hit Nate up for it because I can't cover nearly two thousand dollars on my own. Then there's gas, meals, and equipment, I'm sure.

"No, ma'am. We don't offer payment plans. Maybe you should check with the Y."

"My son wants to play for Mr. Booker."

"Don't they all? Either pay in full or find another program. I'll transfer you to the enrollment director. Good day."

She passes me off so fast, I'm standing with my mouth hanging open.

"Thank you for calling Knights Youth Sports Center. This is Chanel. How may I help you?"

"Chanel?"

"Amber? What's up girl?"

"Trying to decide if I'm pissed or not." I chuckle.

"What happened?"

I fill her in and tell her about my talk with Kemen.

"I thought the football clinic was out or I would have added his name to the scholarship list."

"What are my options now?"

"We take cash, check, or credit card." The tone of her voice changes back as if someone's in her office. "Uh-huh. I got it."

"What's going on over there?" I whisper, leaning into my phone, trying to hear more on the other end.

"Great… great. Have your son here next Friday at seven o'clock for the mandatory orientation. Bring a copy of his shot records, recent physical, and the liability waiver. The address is…"

I'm sitting thoroughly confused.

"Girl, sorry about that. Scarlette's micro-managing ass was standing in my doorway. I'll add him to the roster. Look, I can't get him a scholar-ship, but I can buy you some time. You'll need to pay by the orientation next Friday. That's the best I can do."

"I'll take it. How much time?"

"Wednesday, maybe Thursday at the latest. But this way, I saved his seat."

I exhale. "Okay. I have a week to find fifteen hundred dollars."

"Yes, and his uniform fee. They always have a couple of field trips too. Let me email you the packet." Chanel pecks away on her keyboard and my mind is flooded with the lists of fees. "They'll cover everything during the orientation."

"How much is this going to run me?"

"Roughly three thousand dollars for everything."

"*What?* Did they forget this is a youth clinic?"

"Girl, that's how it is around here. It's like they add extra zeros to keep the regular people out. I only got Brandon in because his program fees are free since I'm an employee. But I have to pay for the other fees out of pocket."

"Damn…" I sing.

"Yep, and I'm family. I wanted to keep Brandon busy since Kemen's going to that engineering camp. Wait, how will he do both?"

"The camp's eight to four."

"Oh, Brandon will be happy to have him on the field."

"Kemen, too. Now, to get the money." I groan. "Thanks, sis."

"You're welcome. Wish I could do more."

"You've bought me time. Now, to call Nate's ass."

"Let him taste it and he'll pass his credit card," she laughs.

"Hell, no. I'm not letting him near my cookie. That's why I'm in this situation now."

I used to give Nate some from time to time. He's a decent lay, and it meant I didn't have to worry about a relationship. Sometimes I don't want a toy and I want to be held. But knowing he has a side piece at every major truck stop just ruined it. I think a part of me held out, waiting for him to change, and I'm not waiting anymore. My days of loving Nate are over. I can trust him with our son, but I can't trust him with my heart.

"Girl, let me get off of this phone. I need to finish up. Want me to grab dinner on the way home?" Chanel brings me back to the issue at hand.

"Yeah. Thank you, girl."

"No problem. Will you keep an eye on Brandon, I want to kick it with Lawrence tonight?"

"You know I will. But Lawrence?"

We have *major* guy issues. I'm the first to admit it. Chanel, on the other hand, loves rocking rose-tinted glasses. Lawrence is a first and fifteenth kind of man— he comes around when she gets paid and he's a ghost when she needs something.

"He's not that bad."

"If you say so." But that ain't my business. We both know she can do better. However, what can I say when I keep letting Nate slip back into my bed? "Just be careful."

"I will."

We disconnect, and I'm left standing with a million micro fires needing my attention. I walk to the porch to check on the boys, and like I thought, they're playing football in the street. They'll play until it's dark, and with Chanel on dinner duty, I'm free to work on the numbers.

I reenter the house. How'd this situation turn upside down in a matter of hours? I pick up my spiral and remember Chanel's email. Our townhouse is small, but it's home. My bedroom holds my queen-size bed and enough furniture to make this my haven. I have a reading chair with an ottoman in one corner and a small desk with my laptop in the other.

I print the clinic packet and climb in my bed to review the program details, and as the total mounts, the walls of my chest squeeze my heart. Will it always be like this? Always barely getting by?

"Stop it, Amber. What's your reality?" I ask myself, looking up at my board with lines and no numbers. I have to give myself something concrete. Feelings aren't facts and freaking out eats at my time. And I don't have enough as it is.

I postpone the pity party and stand at my board. Starting with my paydays and moving to the bills due. These all go in the same color and then I mark those with wiggle room. I move without thinking. This isn't the thinking stage. This is adulting—keeping the lights on and my son fed. It's the price tag for giving my son options.

I stand back. The total exceeds three months of my normal salary. I'm an assistant manager at a family-owned boutique. It doesn't pay much but they give me the flexibility I need to take care of Kemen. They created a special position for me where I oversee all of their Houston locations, which means I can work on the weekends, and late evenings from home. I never have to miss games or practices.

I guess it's time to call my ex.

"What's up, Shorty?"

"Nate."

"Oh hell, what I do now?"

"Nothing yet."

"Are you calling with some bull? Because I got shit to do." He lets about a gruff sigh.

"Kemen was accepted into Jordan Preparatory Academy."

"That's what I'm talkin' about." The pride in his voice brings a smile to my face. "My kid is a fuckin' genius."

"He is. But Nate, he didn't get a scholarship."

"What?"

"He didn't get a scholarship." I repeat, dropping to the foot of my bed. The total stares at me, and I gather my resolve. "Nate, it's seventeen thousand per year."

"For high school?"

"Jordan Prep is the best private school in the city."

Nate mumbles directives to someone, and I hear a door slam on his end. "Listen, Amber, the kid is smart. And I don't have seventeen Gs sitting around. Why can't he go to public school like the rest of us?"

"Because I want better for him."

"Bougie ain't better."

"Broke ain't either."

This is a regular argument for us. I moved across town to get Kemen in a better school district and I put him in "fancy camps", according to Nate. But I want Kemen to see a world without graffiti on the walls, metal detectors at the entrances, and hot boys on the corners. Then I learned about Jordan Prep.

"Nate, we barely get by. I want our son to have his choice of colleges and careers. Not this basic shit we're living."

"Speak for yourself. I own my business."

I wag my head. "Well, since you're balling, why don't you break your son off some."

Nate falls silent. "I will. But I ain't got it. I just bought a new truck and hired a new driver. Things are finally looking up around here."

"It's funny how you always find the money to do what you want, but when it comes to Kemen…"

"Don't do that shit, Amber. I'm building a legacy to give my son and it starts with reinvesting in my business."

"Well, how about investing in your son?"

"That's what I'm doing. I can't grow a business overnight and I can't give you money every time you get a wild hair up your ass. He'll just have to sit this one out."

"Sit this one out?" To say I'm pissed is an understatement. It's like I'm fighting battles everywhere I turn.

"Yeah, I don't have it, and you don't have it. He's smart, he'll be fine, Amber. That boy is a beast on the field. He'll get a scholarship on the strength of that alone."

"And what if he gets hurt? Football isn't guaranteed."

"Neither is a college degree." Nate's voice matches mine.

I hear the front door open and the boys talking. "I gotta go."

"Look, let me get out of here. I'll grab some pizzas and I'll stop by so we can talk about it."

"Nah, we're good." I stand up and tac the acceptance letter on my wall.

"Then text me when Kemen's out for the night."

I laugh. This man done lost his mind.

"What the fuck is so funny?"

"You. Will you at least cover the football camp?"

"Man, I told him—"

"We had a deal. I cover academics and you'll cover sports. Stop acting new." I huff. "Why does it always gotta be a fucking problem to get shit done with you?"

"Because you have your head in the clouds and the rest of us live on earth."

His words feel like a slap. I open my mouth to cuss his ass out, and then I snap it closed.

"Bye, Nate." I disconnect to the sound of him talking in my ear. Kemen will go to Jordan Prep and the football clinic, and I don't need Nate's ass to do it. Now to figure out how.

CHAPTER 3

"Welcome to hot-ass Houston," I mumble, stepping out of the private jet, happy when I see my boys—Kamal Montgomery and Dean Wellington—suited up, leaning against a black Escalade. I'm not from Detroit but I love rolling in a big body and my boys know it.

I smile at the sight. Hands down, these are my brothers, partners in crime. Dead ass. I'd catch a case, raise their kids, throw some hands for them or their families. There's no way I would have entered professional football and no way I'd be here without them. I'll owe these guys until the day I die, but the crew has been infiltrated.

Kamal found Jayda and Dean wifed Baby Miya—Kamal's little sister. I still don't know how that shit went down and the city's still standing. But hey, I have to give it to Dean. He picked well.

I'm the last man standing, and I plan to hold it down for the crew. I got to. And today, DEK Ventures is officially announcing the initiative I've pushed from the day we agreed to become partners in an investment firm. We're launching our first sports clinic for inner city boys.

This shit is about to be epic. I got my boys, we're about to kick off this clinic, *and* I'm back in Houston. I'm about to tear this town up—right after I fuck with them.

"I got Old Man Kamal and Old Man Dean in the flesh. *Whaaaaattttt?*" I lean into it.

Dean's laughing and Kamal's wagging his head.

"Got the old married men, babies daddies, Thing One and Thing Two out of the house. Wait, let me make sure. Jay… Miya…" I call out. "I almost don't recognize ya knuckleheads."

"I'm about to leave your non-funny ass on this runway," Kamal says, pulling me into a hug.

"What's good with you?"

"Man, I'm better than good. I'm blessed. What about you?" Kamal stands back with a smile on his face. He's the glue. We met in junior high, and our friendship has been the most consistent relationship in my life.

"I'm in H-Town with my boys. Does it get any better than that?"

"Nah." Dean responds, and we grasp hands tapping shoulders. He's a smooth brother from another mother and one deck when I need him. Dean gives my back a solid pat, and I pause for a second. "You really about to stare deep into my eyes? I'm sorry, but I'm taken."

"You should leave *his* ass for that wack joke." I glance over, glad to be back with my brothers.

We laugh. This season was long, hard, and disappointing. I got people that I haven't seen in years popping up, asking for money. And we didn't make the playoffs. But I'm back in Houston for the summer and I look forward to hanging with my guys. As for the other clowns trying to play nice, I'm good.

As far as I'm concerned, this is my family. Everyone else is suspect until proven otherwise.

The crew loads my bags in the SUV.

"You driving?" Kamal asks.

"Yeah." He knows I like to drive to get myself back settled into the city. Houston's a unique city. It's a mixture of a big city with a small-town, homey feel. But it never feels like home to me, even though I was born and raised here.

I'm hoping spending the summer here with Kamal and Dean will help me decide if this is the city for me. I have a few more years under my current contract, and I think it might be time for me to join my business partners full time. But for every reason I have to stay, I have another to plant my new life elsewhere.

Kamal tosses the keys and I notice his publicist Ebony. Beautiful dark brown skin beauty. We kicked it a few times. But she's clingy as hell. The second she ran back and told Kamal what went down, I cut her ass off from the D. Kamal's my boy but who I fuck is my business. And he knows how this shit goes.

Before both of them married, we had women in every major city. They retired from playing pro ball and found themselves married with kids. The shit seemed to happen overnight.

I'm upfront with my women and she couldn't respect it, which is a damn shame because I would have liked getting to know her better. But she's watched Kamal and Dean get married and started staring at me with wedding veils in her eyes, and I'm not *that* guy.

Not now, not ever.

I adjust the seat and look over at Kamal in the passenger's seat. "What's on the agenda?"

Ebony pulls out her phone and runs through the day. "We have a meeting with the president and board of Knights Youth Sports Center."

"Scarlette Knight?"

"Yeah. She another one of your conquests?"

My gaze pops to the rearview mirror. "Yep. Why, you mad?"

"You really need to grow up."

"Grow up? You didn't have a problem when I had you climbing the walls, calling my ass daddy." I laugh. "I'll grow up when women stop staring at my dick and my bank account."

"Hoe," she mumbles.

"Don't be mad because you can't ride the ride. Should have kept your mouth closed."

"Children, children." Dean snickers.

Ebony gazes around, and Kamal rubs his eyes in frustration. I can feel the steam coming off of him. This is when men like me get a bad rap. I ignored her since she's Kamal's long-time publicist. But her ebony skin, intelligence, and insistence that I was out of her league made proving her wrong mandatory. Who doesn't love a sexy challenge? Plus, she's around when we run major projects. I thought I'd get the best of both worlds—a beautiful woman on my arm for events and drama-free sex on my off seasons. I got one of the two. She's gorgeous but drama-free she is not.

Now I'm the dog, or a member of the hoe squad because she couldn't follow the rules. And to make matters worse, I have to see her and hear her bitch about me not wanting to settle down. In front of the guys, I'm a hoe, but behind the scenes, she's calling nonstop, flying into town, trying to convince me that she's the woman to change me.

What the fuck? The shit would be laughable if this clinic wasn't my top priority. Now, she's fucking with my business.

"Ebony, is this going to be a problem?" Kamal glances around the seat back at her. "If it is, we understand—"

"But if it is, we can find someone else. This project is too important. Save your petty comments for personal conversations." I add.

Her mouth snaps closed.

"Emmitt," Kamal's stern voice echoes.

"We've negotiated this project for over a year. Everyone down rolls and if she's not down, this ain't the project for her."

The SUV rolls to a stop, and I glance back at her. The guys picked their pet projects. Kamal renovated his family's restaurant—Southern Soul Houston. Dean has us invested in restaurants across the country. We've closed on other joint projects, but this summer, it's finally happening.

My thing is giving back to kids in the foster care system. I want this to be the first of many.

"We've had this conversation in private and you say you're cool. But you're bringing it up again. This is important to me, and I'll find someone else to handle PR if working with me is an issue for you."

"E…" Dean lays a hand on my arm.

But their discomfort doesn't stop my speech. "Nah, Dean, I don't talk to hear myself. I said what I mutha-fuckin' said. We're all adults. This isn't high school. When you play in a big boy's game, you have to play by big boy rules. Period. So, I'll ask again. Ebony, is this a problem?"

"No, Emmitt."

"Thank you."

We ride in silence, and I give her a moment to recover. "How much of my past has Kamal shared?"

"I know a little."

"My mother turned me over to child protective services at twelve years old and never regained full custody of me again. They labeled me an angry Black boy and never placed me in a real home.

"I spent most my youth in group homes. So, this shit is personal. Many of these kids are a number and a paycheck. But we'll give them something different. We can show them their lives and futures matter."

"I'm sorry…"

"Don't feel sorry for me. I made it out. Now we have a chance to extend a hand back. Lord's will, this will be the first of many, so we can't fumble this fuckin' ball, understand?"

A well of emotions stirs inside me. Counseling and real relationships have helped shift my anger to hurt. To handle the drastic shift from living life invisible in people's eyes and, suddenly, they see your ass when you sign a fucking contract.

I feel a hand on my left shoulder and another on my right. This is why I didn't fucking lose it. My anger would drive me to fighting and tearing up whatever I could get my hands on. But now it leads me to give back.

My phone rings and I glance down and it's Robin. I grunt, silencing my phone.

We ride across town. The press conference with Knights Youth Sports Center is scheduled for this afternoon and the orientation with the parents is tomorrow evening. We have less than twenty-four hours to get our portion squared away since we handled the bulk of the decision making virtually.

"What's the final headcount?" I ask Ebony. The last email showed fifty students when I clearly stated I wanted at least one hundred students. It seemed like a nice round number and a benchmark for us to use to evaluate future clinics.

"We're still at fifty. They're open to more, but they have staffing concerns. The more students they accept, you'll need to add dedicated staff for safety reasons."

I nod. "What's the budget like?"

"We've disbursed the known expenses. And you've agreed to fund a portion from your personal charity. So, say the word and we'll work the numbers." Kamal leans against the door.

"Pops is on board for the beverages, lunches, and such. Miya and I will handle the cost for the closing banquet."

"Thanks, man."

"You got it."

"So, our biggest expense is staffing?" I glance over at Kamal.

"Yeah, but that's actually not that bad since all the specialty coaches aren't charging fees." His smile covers his face.

"What do you mean?"

"Everybody agreed to your schedule, and those that had conflicts are sending replacements."

"All from the league?"

"All from the league."

I let his statement wash over me. "Sounds like we have more than enough to show our asses in here."

Dean laughs in the back seat. "We'd expect nothing less from you, brother."

Kamal throws his head back, his shoulders shaking with laughter. "Man, I missed your crazy ass."

"Well, you have eight weeks to get your fill. Anything else I should know, Ebony?"

"Nothing other than most of the press confirmed their presence. I think this would be a great time to mention your desire to partner with other organizations. You'd get a little more press and, hopefully, more nonprofits interested in partnering for future clinics."

I look back at her. "That sounds good. Thanks."

We climb out of the SUV and my phone rings again. I don't bother with checking. "How does she know I'm in town?"

"Might be Mother. They still get together for brunch monthly."

"Why?"

Kamal shrugs. "You know Mother worries about you. When's the last time you two talked?"

"Miss Jackie last week. Robin…" I shrug. She's trying to build a relationship after all of these years. And I'm not falling for it. "I bought her a house and pay her bills. What else do we have to talk about?"

"I'm here if you want to talk." Kamal offers.

"Ain't shit to talk about."

Kamal has a soft spot for my mother because he's a mama's boy. Miss Jackie is nothing like Robin Booker. And that's where Dean and I have an unspeakable bond —we both had mothers that walked away from us.

We stand outside the building and a few news crew vans turn into the parking lot.

"Guys, let's get inside. This will be a good time to address your staffing questions before the reporters arrive." Ebony moves toward the building, and we follow.

"Is that the field we're using?"

"According to the records, it's the only one they have." Ebony says.

I wish I had more time to visit before we start. But the field seems too small to run a full clinic. "Do we still have that contact at Texas Southern University?"

"Yeah, I don't see why not." Kamal says, opening the door for us.

"See if we can use their field."

"I'm on it."

We enter the building, and a small group awaits us. I recognize Scarlette. We met at a mixer Kamal had for Southern Soul a while back.

"Mr. Montgomery, Mr. Wellington, and Mr. Booker."

I tip my head. "It's good seeing you, Scarlette."

"Same to you. We're looking forward to the summer." Her suggestive gaze sweeps over my body as she takes my hand. "Let me give you a quick tour."

We cover the length of the center and I'm concerned with the size. I stop outside the door, looking at the football field. "What's the dimensions of your field?"

"I don't know. But I'm sure Coach Trent knows."

Scarlette takes a few steps and rests a hand on my forearm. "Have you made plans for dinner?"

I look down at her hand, and she removes it. But she's not the kind of woman that stops on the first try. Scarlette is poised, connected, and a great conversationalist. However, she has a jealous streak a mile wide. And her elitist ways don't vibe with the type of people I run with.

I'll never look down on others because I was once like them. I've worked hard to get here, but I know it was nothing but grace and appointed people like Miss Jackie and the Montgomerys who helped me turn my life around.

Scarlette's willingness to let us host this clinic makes me believe there's another layer to her. But she's the kind of person who would ruin a person over some petty shit. All because she can.

To keep my summer drama free, I told the guys I'd leave her alone. I guess I'll have to find other ways to entertain myself since the guys have wives and children now.

I redirect her attention. "How many students are enrolled?"

"We capped at fifty but we have a waiting list."

"How many would we have if you accepted all of those on the waiting list?"

"I'm not sure. We can talk with Chanel, our enrollment director." Scarlette motions back down the hallway.

I look at the guys, and I'm stunned when Ebony doesn't roll her eyes. "If we can do it now, that would help our team prepare for next week."

"Follow me."

CHAPTER 4

"Let me plan a special welcome home night for you."
Scarlette offers the second we're alone.

"I appreciate the offer, but I'm focused on having a
successful clinic. My goal is to make this the first of
many and we wouldn't want to ruin a mutually benefi-
cial endeavor with sex."

Her eyes round. "I thought since you're in town, we
could hang out. See some sights."

"Date?"

"Well, yes, Emmitt. Isn't that what most men your
age want? To find a nice house, a wife, and start
building your family name?"

"I can't speak for most. But this is my legacy." I
glance down the hallway as the others enter the auditorium. Scarlette and I had dinner, and the sex wasn't

memorable—neither good nor bad. She was just a way to pass the time while the guys were occupied with their wives.

I look over at her. "You're a beautiful woman, and I'm sure you'll make some man an excellent wife, but you're barking up the wrong tree. I told you how I roll. Dinner and a nice night cap and I'm good. But I'm not the guy you want to hang your hat on."

"I disagree."

I chuckle. "Will this be a problem? Because we plan to invest our time and efforts into your organization, your father begged us to do it here. But I'm having second thoughts."

"Emmitt, you're exactly where you need to be. Just give me a chance to show you." She runs a hand over my tie and smiles seductively. "I know people, and if you decide to make Houston your home, we could run this city. I'm much more than a pretty face. But there's no need to answer me now, we have the entire summer."

Scarlette turns and stops outside an office and knocks on the door. Then lets herself inside.

"Chanel, this is Mr. Booker with DEK Ventures. He has some questions about the wait list."

Chanel stands with her eyes round, but she recovers quick. I shake her hand and Scarlette's called to the conference room.

"I can find my way back." I assure her. Then she's off. Chanel and I sit. "I'd like to start with the number of students on the waiting list."

Chanel pulls up to her computer and starts typing. "We have forty-seven students on the waitlist."

"I thought we'd have more interested."

"You've attracted students that rarely participate in Knights programs. But many withdrew their applications because of financial reasons. Will you offer scholarships? If so, we have these students too." Chanel withdraws a stack of applications.

"Can you reach out to those students and invite them to the orientation?"

"Sure, I can email them."

"Would you?"

"Yes, my son and godson love you." She swipes her hand back and forth as if flustered before returning to her computer. "You're their favorite player."

"You'll have to bring him up and introduce him. But you don't look old enough to have a teenager."

"Well, I do, and I will." She counts through the other applicants. "You'll sit somewhere around a hundred and seventy-five if everyone attends."

I nod, calculating the figures in my head. "Miss Knight mentioned student ratios. How many coaches would I need to accept all of those students?"

"The state average is seventeen to one. We don't

have to stick to those ratios. But the closer you do, the more you can spot issues."

"Do you have coaches on staff for the summer?"

"Normally, yes. Let me give you the contact information for Coach Trent. He handles our outdoors sports programs."

"That would be perfect."

Chanel scribbles details on a notepad and passes it to me. "Is there anything else I can help you with?"

"Mr. Booker." We look towards Scarlette in the doorway. "The reporters are ready."

"Okay. I'll be right there. Chanel, thank you." I stand. "I appreciate your help and it was a pleasure meeting."

She takes my hand. "I think it's really amazing that you guys are doing this." She lifts the folder. "And I'll take care of this before I leave."

I nod, "Please, don't forget to bring your son over."

"I will. But don't blame me if they fan boy out."

"I won't." I turn to follow Scarlette. The guys and I have more to discuss but Chanel armed me with the information I need to help as many kids as possible. I know how I'll use the extra budget we have.

"Lights, cameras, action," I whisper, buttoning my jacket before we enter the conference room. I hold the door open for Scarlette and guide her inside with a light hand on her lower back. The reporters stand, turning their cameras in our direction.

Goddamn! I'm about to do this shit.

The door closes behind us and heads turn. Many reporters pop to their feet as I walk down the center aisle. I acknowledge familiar faces, turning on every bit of influence I have in my being. My heart's eager to race ahead. I could execute a mean back flip and wave on their asses, but the significance of this moment humbles me.

The orphan. The chocolate kid with the nappy hair and skinny legs. The Black boy with the attitude. He did this. He made this happen.

Right here. Right now. I can't make this shit up. But I willed it. I knew I would be here.

A reel of every yard, every football field, and every signed contract flashes before my eyes. And then I see thirteen-year-old Emmitt watching life throw shots.

Moms gave me up. My Dad is unknown. Teachers sentenced me to a future of poverty with their words. I slept in a room with over twenty other boys like me. Now many of them are locked up, but this dream kept me sane.

The dream of a room full of reporters waiting to talk with me. That people would know my name before I opened my mouth. That my name would be associated with good and not harm, philanthropy and not crime. That everyone who dissed on me would regret sleeping on Emmitt Booker.

But I won't use this time to gas myself up. I'm about to flip this shit until the world is full of second chances like me. And it starts with a seed. If I sow hope, then I'll reap a field of possibility, prosperity, and promise.

Yeah… I like that shit. This will be the source of my harvest.

"Good morning!" My voice fills the room, and every head turns. A few reporters stand, extending hands in my direction. I shake them, thank them for their presence. I continue until I stop at the front table.

I bump fists with Kamal and then Dean and pull out the chair for Scarlette next to Ebony. I lower behind the microphone. Lights flash and we sit for a few minutes. I direct my gaze at the heart of the lenses. These are the people who will rain on my field and help us spread the message.

I bow my head for a moment and pray, *May my offering be pleasing and acceptable in Your sight.* Then I lean forward and face the main camera.

"Thank you all for coming out. I'm Emmitt Booker. My business partners, Kamal Montgomery and Dean Wellington, are proud to announce the first sports clinic hosted by DEK Ventures. And we decided to host it right here in our hometown, Houston, Texas."

For twenty minutes, I share the vision of DEK Ventures sports clinics and the imprint we aim to make in the country. We answer questions as the reporters seize the opportunity to talk with three professional athletes turned moguls, and we've done it together.

"Emmitt, you are *the man* after signing a five-year contract with Dallas. Does this mean you'll join Kamal and Dean in retirement?" a reporter asks.

"No, I'm looking forward to the season. But we know football isn't a long-term plan. It's wise to have options."

"You all invest in restaurants, real estate, a few start-ups. Why the pivot to sports clinics? Besides the obvious," a report on the front rows asks.

Dean leans into the microphone. "We have several reasons. The first is that's how we met. I doubt our paths would have crossed. We all lived very different lives, but on the field, we were the same."

"And we needed to find the right venue. I'm based here, thanks to Southern Soul, and Dean's recently moved back, so he's here as well. It felt right for all of us to do this project at home together." Kamal adds.

"But we had a missing link." I pick up. "We needed the *right* location. We needed Knights Youth Sports

Center. Thanks to some good southern food and a few drinks, we connected with Mr. Knight. His legacy continues with his daughter, Scarlette Knight. She's graciously opened their center to us and we're ready to give these young kings an experience unmatched."

Scarlette tosses me a wink and I smile, redirecting my attention to the reporters.

The press conference closes, and we mingle with the staff for a few minutes before Scarlette wraps a hand around my arm to gain my attention.

"You're a pro," she purrs. "The reporters loved you."

"You doubted?" I lift a brow and she giggles. "We'll be here for the orientation. But I'm interested in filling the camp. Can I count on you to make it happen?"

"Absolutely. How about we discuss it further, maybe tonight, my place?"

I would have been surprised if she didn't try again. Gone are the days when women understand a good time is a good time. Nothing more. And like Ebony, Scarlette doesn't know how to play by the rules. "We have other matters to handle this afternoon. How about we arrive a half hour before the orientation?"

Her smile falls flat. "Uh yeah, sure."

"Great. We'll see you tomorrow." I lean in and kiss her cheek.

The disapproving look on her face makes me hold back my chuckle. I'm drawing the line but I'm not stupid. Her little speech earlier shows I'll have to tread lightly. I need her invested in our success and we're guests in her house. Scarlette holds the keys.

We silently leave and climb into the SUV. The next stop, we leave Ebony at the hotel, and we end at Q's Spot for drinks.

Kamal's the oldest Montgomery sibling. He has four brothers—Rashaad, Demetrius, and Quan—and a sister, Miya. Quan is the youngest. He's also the owner, boisterous host, and the "Q" in Q's Spot. He's also Kamal's youngest brother. His team sets up a VIP room and we relax to talk shop. They decorated the room like a lounge with plush couches with a private bar and a dedicated waitstaff. The music plays softly, and the low lighting makes the room have a chill vibe.

We order a round of beers and sit back to discuss the press conference. I sit on one end of the couch and Kamal on the other.

"My biggest concern is reaching at least a hundred students." I say, ready to get rid of this suit and tie. My preferred attire is casual clothes but today I made an exception.

"You will if all the students show tomorrow. Right?" Dean says, lounging in the chair to my right.

"Yes, but only if they can afford it." I convey the details shared by Chanel.

"How much is the camp, anyway?" Kamal asks.

We set this up under the Knights' general program. The center handles registration, insurance, the location, as normal. We're in place to handle the specialty staffing and I'll oversee the training for the full eight weeks.

I pull up the packet Chanel emailed me, swiping through the pages until I see the registration form. "Fifteen hundred dollars!"

"You've got to be kidding me." Kamal says, grabbing my phone.

"This can't be normal. Is it normal?"

"It sounds expensive to me." Dean runs a hand over his face.

"Let me call Jay." Kamal passes my phone back. He takes a few minutes on the call with his wife.

Money shouldn't be the reason a child can't enroll in our clinic. "I hated not participating in programs because I didn't have money. Football was my ticket from poverty, and it gave me a platform to change my life. How can we do the same?"

"Here, here, brother." Dean tips his beer in my direction.

Then I remember Chanel gave me Trent's number. I call with him and invite him to join us for drinks. Thankfully, he accepts. I'm hopeful between Chanel and Trent we might get a real insight into the Knights setup.

"What's the goal?" Kamal asks, sitting back while we wait.

"Besides running a successful clinic?"

"Yeah, you need to define it. Start with the end in mind."

I sit back, running through the schedule. But the financial concern commands my attention. "I think I want to scrap the tuition issue."

"What do you mean?" Dean asks.

"I think we should cover the tuition." I look between them. "I don't care how long it's been since we attended summer camps. Fifteen hundred was expensive then, and it's expensive now."

Kamal takes a drag of his beer. "Jay thinks it's expensive but when you divide it over eight weeks, it's pretty normal for a good program."

"But to require it up front?" I throw out, shaking my head. "The goal is to give them access to something different. It's about the football but it's not. And we can't do that if they're not in the room."

I look between them and continue, "We can spit the PC facts on the mic, but I want these young men to see themselves in us. That their horizons are wider because they see these successful Black men coaching them."

"What's your gut saying?" Dean asks. "We have the

budget. If we don't, we can find the funds. But we'll have to insert a clause for future organizations to keep the program fees commensurate with their existing rates."

"I like the sound of that. Especially when we're covering equipment, food, and the coaches. What are they charging for?"

"Nonprofits are a big business." The words come from a man in the doorway. "Trent Cooper."

I stand. "Emmitt Booker, and this is—"

"Kamal and Dean. I'm a fan. Nice to meet you all."

"What can I get you, man? A beer?"

"Yeah, that sounds good."

Trent takes the seat in the vacant chair.

"Tell me about yourself." I ask, trying to see if we have an ally in this situation.

He's from Houston, went to the University of Houston. Played college football.

"Are you working for the Knights Center full time?"

"Not this summer since you guys are running the camp. Miss Knight said the hiring and firing would be at your discretion. So, I had to let my staff go."

"What? How many coaches?" A knot forms in my stomach.

"I was the only full-time staff, but I had part-time college and high school students, which caused a disturbance at the Center."

"How so?" Kamal asks.

"Miss Knight cut everyone except essential staff until the fall."

"Why would she do that?" I ask, not liking what I'm hearing.

"It's cheaper."

His words feel like a sharp pain in my chest. Do we cover the tuition or rehire the staff? I don't want to make that choice. The students need help, and the coaches should have the option to work with us.

I need the guys alone to work this out. But Trent shouldn't lose his job because we're hosting this clinic. That just doesn't feel fair.

"Trent, how do you feel about working with me for the summer?"

"I'd be honored." Trent says without hesitation.

"And your coaches, do you think they'd want to join us for the summer? I can only speak for the next eight weeks."

"I'm sure most of them will jump at the chance. This would be a great resume builder for the students. And we all can learn a little from the pros."

"Man, I like the way you think. Can you put the word out to your coaches? Have them meet us tomorrow after the orientation and we'll work it out."

"Man, thank you." He stands and gives me a firm handshake.

"You're welcome. We'll see you tomorrow."

Trent leaves and the guys exchange glances.

"What about Scarlette?" Dean asks. "I don't like the way she rolls." Dean whispers, and I agree.

"And I don't like that she didn't mention it to us." Kamal looks over at me. "You're running this show, but it seems like bad blood to fire the local staff and bring in professional athletes."

I nod, weighing the options. Her execution is shady as fuck. I sit down and open the cigar box on the table.

"We'll surprise the shit out of her ass at the orientation and keep our eyes open."

Dean chuckles. "My man."

"Kamal?"

"I'm down. What about the scholarships?"

I almost forget about our plan to offer an academic scholarship. Quick math will put us on the hook for almost two hundred students and at least fifteen coaches plus Trent. But we don't have meals or the fees for the specialty coaches.

"We'll do that too. Let me sleep on it and we'll talk about it in the morning. For now, I'll get us another round before I send you old men home to your wives and I find some entertainment for the night."

They laugh and we kick back, falling into our usual mode. I light another cigar and hold up my glass. "To an eventful summer. Dean with a little one on the way. Kamal and his growing family."

"Emmitt with football and his fuckboy summer."

Our laughter fills the room, and we celebrate another successful DEK project. I've missed hanging with my boys.

"Look, just because you retired your jersey gives you no right to shit on mine."

Dean holds his side. "Man, you need to find you one good one. It will change your life."

"Oh, hell nawl! For the record, y'alls asses broke the pact. We said no wives and no kids. This one," I point at Kamal, "has not one but two crumb-snatchers."

"And I ain't shamed. *Shiiiitttt*, my wife would have most men drooling and that's after having two kids."

"That's not the point. The point is how am I supposed to kick it with my boys and y'all got curfews." Kamal can't say shit, and Dean can't either. "And this one is minutes from changing your life."

"Man, tell me about it. I still can't believe I'm about to be a father." Dean sits back with a goofy smile on his face. "Curfews aren't all bad."

"Dean… Don't say something stupid about my sister." Kamal points a finger in his direction, and I'm hollering.

"Baby Miya ain't Baby Miya anymore. She's my wife and about to be the mother of my child."

"*Ooooohhhhh*... Your boy is throwing receipts up in this bitch." I instigate. I have to, it's how I keep the festivities rolling. "I still don't know how you pulled that shit off. Had King Kamal about to blow a fuse over his sister."

Dean pulled off the heist of the year. Marrying and now having a kid with Kamal's sister. The boy is smooth.

"Man, what can I say, your boy still got it." Dean adds and Kamal's on his feet.

"Just because she's your wife doesn't mean I won't bust your ass."

I fall back on the couch. "No ass busting allowed. You might throw a hip."

"Man, fuck you." He chuckles, glances at his watch. "Man, I need to run if I want to read Reese a bedtime story."

"There goes the neighborhood." I throw up my hands.

"Yeah, I need to bounce, too. Miya gave me a list of snacks to get from the store. I live in the grocery store." Dean wags his head, throwing some cash on the table. "Because a pregnant professional chef wants nothing but junk food."

"And this is what happens when my boys get wives." I rock my head in mock disgust, but I'm proud of my boys. "One more shot for the road."

We stand and we toss back shots before pounding fists and hugging.

"Yo, where's Q? Because he always knows where the party's at."

Yeah, this summer will be dope. Now to find some hot girls to fulfill my *fuckboy summer*.

CHAPTER 5

"Ma, we can't be late." Kemen insists. We're late but not super late.

"Kemen, these things never start on time." I tell my anxious son. "Call Aunt Chanel and put her on speakerphone."

He dials, and I focus on the road. I'm not a dime closer to paying for this clinic since Nate's dodging my calls. Then he texted Kemen saying he's doing an across country trip. I shake my head, watching for kids in the street and cops. This sista deserves a set of wings because I'm flying.

"Where are you?" she yells over the noisy background.

"Up the street. Save us a seat."

Kemen chuckles. We're not on the block or in the neighborhood, but close enough.

"You must want me to throw some bows in here."

I laugh and grab the phone, pressing it to my ear. "What?"

"You'll see when you get here. This place is packed, and the kids didn't come to play."

My car is floating like a big body Cadillac, and I exhale, seeing the center up ahead. "Have they started?"

"No, there seems to be a little misunderstanding. I think Mr. Booker's about to set Scarlette straight."

"Girl, I don't have time for gossip. We're coming in hot. Save our seats. Bye." I hang up, whipping into the parking lot on two wheels, sliding into the first available space. "Thank you, Jesus. We made it in one piece. Now, get the paperwork."

We work in tandem, crossing each other into the backseat. Kemen jumps out, runs around the car, opening my door and I snatch up my purse.

"Thank you, baby." I use my reflection to straighten my clothes.

"Ma!" He opens the door and puts on his jacket.

"I'm coming." I smooth out my skirt over my hips and flip my microlocks to the side. When I spin around and notice his tie. "Come here, let me fix your tie."

My handsome son selected a suit and tie for his meetings today. We started at the orientation for the engineering camp and now we're here. His curly fro hawk is on point, thanks to Brandon. And I almost giggle when I see Kemen left that little peach fuzz on his chin.

"Do you think you'll need to change your clothes?" I pat his chest to signal I'm all done.

"No, ma'am. It wasn't on the schedule. But I have my gym bag in the trunk, just in case."

We run across the parking lot, and the silence tells me the meeting must be underway. He points to the auditorium.

"Look for Aunt Chanel."

Kemen nods, and I slowly open the door. The room is full, and it's hard to see across the sea of people. The chairs face a stage, but it's the man pacing in front that's holding their attention.

"She's right there." Kemen moves and I nod, intending on following him when my eyes settle on the speaker.

I stumble to a full stop, and his dark gaze sweeps my body. A parade of fairies flutters in my stomach. The picture did him no justice. The hue of his dark skin, the curls on the tip of his fade, the sharp trim of the goatee. It takes no skill on my part to imagine what he's working with under that suit as I let my eyes crawl the length of his body.

"Pardon me," I whisper. He tips his head and returns his attention to the crowd, freeing me to follow

Kemen. And I'll be damn, *why did Chanel's ass pick that seat?*

I stop, searching the crowd for another seat. But see nothing. Now, I have to walk to the front of the auditorium and sit my ass in the front row.

Fuck me! I stop at the end of the aisle, waiting for him to pass. He comes up beside me, attracting the attention of the others.

"Running a little late, Miss…"

"Evans … Amber Evans. I apologize. Our last appointment ran late."

"I'm a stickler for timeliness. The game waits for no one." He steps closer, bringing his damn scent, and my vajayjay purrs.

Oh shit, now.

Goddamnit, this ain't the time, my inner voice demands. But my heart's thumping like my ass learned to play the damn Congo drums, and he's trying to hold a conversation. My eyes dart to Kemen because I know he's petrified.

"My apologies. I'll keep that in mind, Mr. Booker."

A soft groan reaches my ear and our eyes lock. He steps closer. "Emmitt."

"What?"

"Coach Emmitt."

I tip my head, acknowledging his words, not

trusting myself to speak. Then he motions in front of him toward my seat. "After you."

I swear a smile lingers in Coach Emmitt's eyes, as if he can sense my uneasiness. I'm tired and I had to drive across town and all I want is to sit my ass in that seat. Seconds feel like hours, and we're at a standstill. Everyone is staring at us, and he doesn't seem pressed to move on until he's good and ready.

"Fine." I roll my eyes, and he chuckles until I cross his path. The sharp intake of his breath sends my gaze back to him. Unmistakable fire burns in his eyes and a challenge lurks in their depths.

I return my attention to my short walk, giving Coach Emmitt an eyeful. Tastefully, I wear my size sixteen well. Every curve on display, from my wide hips to my thick thighs and my bubble ass.

My son asked me to dress up, he wanted "my fly to match his fly." And I didn't bark because my kid likes to turn heads on and off the field. You'd know him in a crowd even if he wasn't the star player on every team. He's that kid. So, I selected a silk blouse, coral skirt, and nude heels.

I lower into my chair, fully aware of the daggers aimed at me. And I'll bet the ringleaders are the gorgeous women sitting with two men behind a table— one with ebony skin, the other with fairer skin. The latter looks familiar. I wonder if that's Chanel's cousin.

I toss Coach Emmitt a wink, and he chuckles and resumes his presentation.

"Well, hello diva," Chanel whispers.

"What do you expect when you sit in the front row?" I wiggle trying to get comfortable in my seat.

"I wanted to smell the essence of rich." Her ridiculous voice sounds like Strange's from the movie *Boomerang*.

"Your ass is a nut," I whisper back. Then Coach Emmitt walks by and she takes a deep inhale, and so do I. "Girl, that ain't rich you smell, that is S-E-X-Y."

"Ma!" Kemen chimes in.

"Fine." I hold up my hands in surrender, then turn and listen to the presentation.

I watch Mr. Booker, aka Coach Emmitt, aka Sexy AF walk back and forth, and I can't focus because I'm mesmerized watching him come and go. The cut of his suit. The shine of his shoes. The way he talks with his hands. And oh my god, his scent. Rich, sexy, whatever it is lingers, and the hum between my thighs vibrates through my body.

Men are low on my list of priorities. Nate sort of blew my fascination with the institution of "us"—a couple agreeing to face life together. It wasn't our lack of money or our lack of education or our struggle to raise a child with no experience. It was the lies, his infidelity. He had women popping up at our house, I had a bitch in my face at my job. And I'm not about calling a queen out of her name, but she showed up at my place of employment asking about *my* man. She wanted her ass kicked.

I'm one step out of the hood and I'm not above acting a fool. But that was it for me. I literally couldn't take it. I can do bad on my lonesome. Nate was gone more than he was home. And when he was home, we argued nonstop, and I was stressed the fuck out.

The stress caused me to eat. The more I ate, the more my hips spread. The more my hips spread, the more he cheated. In all of my grandness, I was never enough, and somewhere over the years, it became easier to focus on Kemen. I can handle football practice and magnet programs and teenage emotions. What I can't handle is raising a grown-ass man. It's easier pushing to get my kid in an Ivy League university than trying to understand the minds of men.

Coach Emmitt stops in front of the audience. I wonder what his type is. Tall, thin, weave, natural. His eyes find mine and I face the front. He could be one of those guys who has a big girl fantasy. *I hate those.*

Applause fills the room, and I snap out of my stupor. I'm sitting in the front row, daydreaming about a man that is outside my reach. Not because I doubt myself. I'm a fucking catch—most days. But my life is a hot-ass mess. I'm the layaway queen. I have enough gas to get us home and beyond that, my priority is finding the dough to pay for this clinic and staying away from Coach Emmitt.

Yeah, that's a smart decision. I nod my head. Who needs a fine ass, sexy coach? Not me. What I need is a bubble bath, a cheeseburger, and a Diet Coke. Cause I'm not trying to blow my entire diet.

I look down at Chanel's journal and smile. "Girl, I'm going to need your notes."

"I got you."

Coach Emmitt reclaims his seat, staring at me.

"I can't do this." I hiss from the side of my mouth to Chanel.

"That man likes what he sees," she mumbles behind her hand. "But I think someone is *salt-tee*." Chanel tips her head to the fairer skinned woman.

My suspicion about the identity is confirmed once she stands behind the podium. Scarlette Knight welcomes the parents and students. And she's about to close out the meeting when Coach Emmitt hops to his feet.

"Thank you, Miss Knight. Let's give her another round of applause. And as a token of our gratitude my business partners and I have a surprise. Kamal, Dean." The other delectable men sitting behind the table join Emmitt, flanking Miss Knight. "In exchange for your generosity, we are covering the tuition of every student present tonight."

My heart drops, and my gaze snaps to Coach Emmitt, and he winks. I clap with the others. The kids are jumping up and down, and I drop back in the chair.

"But wait, there's more," Emmitt continues. "The amazing Miss Knight agreed to offer three full academic scholarships."

The three men clap their hands with all of us. But Scarlette looks like she's pissed. My eyes slide to Emmitt's *gotcha* expression.

"Oh, they got her ass," Chanel giggles.

"What do you mean?" I'm searching the faces of people in front of us, and the tension is evident on Miss Knight's face. "Can they do that?"

Chanel shrugs, "I don't see why not."

"But that's a good thing. Right?"

"Does this mean we get a refund?" someone from the back calls out.

"Absolutely." Emmitt answers, and Scarlette turns white. I've never seen a Black woman turn ghost white. To be honest, it's kind of scary. "Chanel, could you give us a hand? Everyone that paid, meet her at the back table. Young Kings, let's huddle up in the back right corner."

Chanel goes one way, Kemen goes another. The energy in the room is contagious. I sit back in the chair, relieved to scratch the clinic fee off my list. But I'm not in the clear.

I have questions about the scholarships, but I see Scarlette in a heated discussion with Emmitt. He stands with his hands draped casually in his pockets. I look back and see Kemen with the other players. Chanel left her notes on the chair. I grab them and start transcribing to my pad.

I fill two sheets of paper with my scribbles. The camp is eight weeks, and it's a specialty clinic. The coaches cover technique, nutrition, mental health—which surprises me. They'll have scrimmages. The first two weeks are more like an audition to complete the final six weeks.

I wonder how the scholarships will factor in. Is it a college scholarship or can we use it for private school? The trickle of awareness sprinkles down my spine. What if Kemen could land one? It means I wouldn't have to work extra hours or find a second job. But it wouldn't be a guarantee.

"Hold your horses, take one win at a time." I remind myself.

"That doesn't sound like fun."

My head snaps up and I look back at the boys waiting in the corner and back to Emmitt. "Do you make it a habit of moving at your own pace?"

"Says the woman that was late."

"We were stuck in traffic."

"Leave early."

The electricity between us feels life changing. That I was meant to meet this man.

"Coach Emmitt, we need to discuss this. The nonprofit can't—"

"Miss Knight, do you want us here?"

"Yes."

"Then make it work."

Scarlette's mouth snaps shut.

"Now, if you'll excuse us." Emmitt faces me, dismissing Scarlette.

She walks away, and I follow her until she reaches the center aisle.

"That was… *harsh*." I glance over at him.

"That's life."

"Well, damn. Do you need a hug?" I chuckle.

"Maybe, are you giving them out?" His voice sounds like velvet.

"So, you're just going to shoot your shot?"

"Hell, yeah." His head falls back, and his easy laugh has me joining in.

"No, sir, not happening. But I appreciate your generosity."

"You're welcome. And thank you for wearing that skirt." His eyes sweep down my body.

Heat floods my face. This man has no chill and I think I like it. "Coach, your team is waiting."

"My team is waiting," he repeats, taking a few steps backwards. "I'm look forward to getting one of those hugs, Amber Evans."

"Your team…"

And with a two-finger salute, Emmitt Booker leaves me standing, and like a woman asking for trouble, I watch that gorgeous man walk away. He enters the center of the huddle and I move to return to my seat, and Scarlette's staring me down.

What was that?

Sis doesn't have a problem with me because I'm not here to find a man. All I need is my baby on the field and the rest is none of my damn business.

I pull out my phone, and text Nate, *Kemen's clinic is covered. But his tuition is due on August 1st.*

He called this morning, promising to help. I'll believe it when I see it. His ass is Casper the Ghost when I need him, and the cheering father when the shit's handled.

"We solved the problem, let that shit ride." I tell myself, dropping my notebook back in my purse.

I'll meet you in the car, I text Kemen and head to my car. I think this celebration calls for a burger, fries, and a regular Coke. I'll celebrate tonight and create a plan to pay for Jordan Preparatory Academy tomorrow.

CHAPTER 6

AMBER APPROACHES the edge of the field. I notice her every move, not because she's late to every practice, but because she's drop-dead gorgeous with her curvy body. And her eyes, her amber eyes, won't save her today.

"What time is it, Coach?"

"Half past. What do you want to do?" Coach Trent stands beside me.

The boys are warming up on the field, and Kemen is late. I have no tolerance for tardiness, but I extend a grace period to the boys since they're not responsible for driving themselves. The parents signed contracts concerning their attendance to play and be candidates for the scholarships.

Kemen Russell isn't an ordinary kid. He has a mixture of raw talent, speed, and he's a natural leader. The others move when he moves. He's a rare lump of coal needing the right environment to form into his full potential. Because this kid could go all the way. But I can't help him if he's late.

"Sideline him. Run the drill again and I'll be right back." I stroll over, giving myself time to feast on Amber. She must have come straight from work, judging by her clothes. The skirt reminds me of the peach number she wore to the orientation.

Kemen stops at the chalk line. "Coach E."

"Young King." We bump fists. I extend the respect I expect, and this kid doesn't disappoint. I cross my arms over my chest, staring him straight in the eyes. "I don't want to do this. You're one of my best players. But you can't practice today."

"Yes, sir. I know. I just wanted my teammates to know I'm here."

"I respect that. How old are you?"

Kemen's gaze doesn't waver. He has his mother's eyes but not her height. The kid must be close to six feet, and I can tell he hits the gym, yet another example of his discipline. So, I have to find a way to help him.

"Thirteen, sir."

"Coach E, they're ready." Trent calls out.

I nod and face Kemen. "You can join the huddle, but you can't play."

"Thank you, sir."

"Head over, I'll be right there."

Amber smacks her lips, rolling her beautiful golden eyes. I look down at her. After openly flirting with her and pissing Scarlette off, I promised myself I'd stay away from parents of the boys. And I know Scarlette only cares because this energy between Amber and I is that apparent.

I agreed, and Scarlette signed off on funding three academic scholarships at the end of the clinic. In exchange, she's texted me and showed up at practice almost daily, inviting me to one social event or another. Scarlette wants to introduce me to her elite friends. I know how that shit works. She gets seen on my arm and I meet the affluent socialites in Houston.

Scarlette comes from what we call old money. Her father is a football Hall of Famer and her mother's family has ties to Texas oil. I'm sure meeting her friends would benefit us later, but her actions have red flags all over her situation. But I might have to take one for the team to make this clinic run smoothly. That means having drinks with Scarlette and keeping my distance from Amber.

Kemen steps back and kisses the top of his mother's head. The gesture surprises me. Most teenage boys wouldn't openly show affection, but these two are an odd pair. Amber whispers something and he nods before running off.

"It's not his fault." She steps forward and I stare down at her, torn. "I'm driving, blame me."

"Tardy players can't touch this field. You signed a contract." I remind her, and I've never wanted to kiss a woman more than I want to kiss Amber. And I can't put my finger on what it is. Yeah, she's beautiful, and the sight of her fully clothed makes my dick hard. But there's more to her.

"But life isn't on your contract. I have to go to work, pick him up from camp, and get him here. I'm only one person." Amber uses her hands to iterate her point. She's trying to hand me my ass because she was late. Yet all I see are the tops of her full breasts jiggling with each move.

A groan lodges in my throat as my hormones spaz. It's over a hundred degrees out here, and after standing in the hot-ass sun, I'm tired. My head drops back, counting the hours until it's Friday.

"Damn, at least look at me when I'm talking to you. Walking around in those shades like you're a celebrity."

I respect her request, opening my eyes and I glance down.

"Miss Evans, I'm not here to manage your schedule. That's not on me. I'm trying to teach these boys responsibility. Football is a dangerous sport."

"I'm cool with that, but you don't have to be so

cold about it. Kemen shouldn't be penalized for my mistake."

"I'm not cold. I'm coaching your son. Which I can't do if he's late. There are no excuses on the field. Tardiness means they're distracted. Distractions lead to injuries. I need his head in the game." I take a step closer and immediately regret it. The tips of her perky breast brush my chest and we're both taken aback by the chemistry passing between us. So, I step back. "Miss Evans, your inability to manage your schedule puts every child on that field at risk. Instead of being pissed at me, buy a watch. Either get your son here on time or find another program."

I turn to join the huddle, furious and itching to see the very beautiful Amber Evans in action. It must be the heat that has me delirious. I need to go out tonight. I've been eating, sleeping, living on this field. We had to get new equipments, new field posts, and an upgrade in the locker room. I thought I agreed to coach a team, and it's become an overhaul of their entire football program.

"You better be glad my son begged to play for you." Her sly words reach my ears and I hit an about face.

It only takes me four steps to get back to her. Amber stares up at me with storms brewing in her eyes. Where her son is tall, she's only a few inches over five feet. This angle gives me a perfect view of her distracting breasts. This woman is pissed, and I want to run my tongue across her mounds.

"Care to repeat that, Miss Evans?" She shifts from one leg to the other, and I swear on god, I could take her on this field. "And before you answer, remember I'm a grown ass man."

"What the hell is that supposed to mean? I'm trying to put you up on game. Take that monkey off your back."

"Is that right?" I step closer. "And what is it *you* think *I* need, Amber?" Her eyes widen, her lips part, and I smile, wondering if she's this passionate in the bed.

"Don't smile yet. Ain't nothing changed."

"You sure about that?" We're so close, her breasts brush my chest with each inhale. We have a crowd, and I don't give a damn. This showdown is inevitable between her tardiness and our sexual tension. "I'm waiting."

"On what?" Amber's tongue sweeps across her bottom lip. *Yeah, ya boy's still got it.*

"You said something about putting me up on game."

And with an attitude that only a sista can give, she rests her hands on those wide hips, not backing down. "You need to get laid."

"Are you offering?"

Her gasp hangs between us. I lower my head until my mouth lingers by her ear. "Your ass talk big game. Name the time and place and I got you."

Amber laughs, and my shit is instantly hard. She turns up those tempting lips, nailing me with those eyes. "I said get laid, not change your fucking life cause it don't get no better than this."

I stare down at her, and she knows what time it is. It would take less than an inch to sample her sassy mouth. The only thing keeping us vertical and not horizontal are my players on the field. I know it. She knows it. Then she wisely turns, and all I can do is stare at all that ass.

"You're playing with fire," I yell.

"It's all good. I got insurance." She winks and heads to the bleachers.

"What was that?" I look over, surprised to see Dean.

"Man, fuck if I know. Come on, let's talk with the players."

I use the walk to the huddle to clear my head. Amber's words felt like an erotic dare, but she's Kemen's mother. Thank god, Dean's the special coach today.

"Take a knee." I wait for them to settle around me, and my eyes find Amber in the crowd. What am I going to do about her? About Kemen on this team?

About this frustration mounting every time Amber and I are alone?

"E, you good?" Dean whispers.

"Yeah, man." I shake that shit off. "Young Kings, I have my boy and best friend here to run drills. Our focus today is on safety. How we run, how we hold the ball, how we execute our plays.

"We love this game, but we love our brothers more. And as our brother's keeper, we ensure the safety of the team. Understand?"

"Sir, yes, sir," echoes around me.

"So we play smart, we play safe, and we play skilled. The goal is to enjoy the game and walk off the field. Understand?"

"Sir, yes, sir."

"Remember, this is our second week. This is the last week to run basic drills. Tryouts start Monday. Those that make the cut will finish the rest of the camp. I believe all of you have the talent to do it." My gaze lingers on Kemen. "Coach Dean."

I step back, and Dean steps forward. I give Kemen a slight nod and he excuses himself. Amber pops to her feet and I can feel her eyes on me.

The energy between us is explosive. We're at each other's throats and I can't fuck her and move on. Not with her kid on my team. That's what's wrong with Scarlette and Ebony. No matter how many times, or how many languages I use, they still think they'll change my mind. I'm not husband material. It's not my calling, nor do I want it to be. I'm here for six more weeks and I'm back to Dallas. But Amber's cocky comeback makes me want to prove her wrong. I'll have her ass calling me daddy with those juicy ass thighs thrown over my shoulders.

A little voice whispers, *What if she's right?* I chuckle. That shit ain't happening. Women come and women go, that's how it goes. I enjoy them while I have them and wish them well when they leave.

I plant myself to watch the offense and defense run drills passing between the teams when I'm stopped in my tracks once again by Amber and Kemen. Once dismissed from the group, he didn't sit on the bleachers, like other players have done, and he didn't sit on the sideline. Kemen started running the length of the field.

I watched as the two went back and forth until Amber stormed off, and I thought she left, but she returns in gym shoes. Then she joined her son running the perimeter of the field in a skirt. She struggled but didn't stop until they started passing the ball. I've never seen a mother and son behave the way they do, and I can't pull my eyes away.

Now they're at the end of the field, Amber catches the ball, fakes a pass, rolling around her son then she steps into the end zone and hits a swag and surf.

"Yo, E?"

"What's up, man?" I grip hands with Kamal and tap shoulders, not taking my eyes off them because I can't take my eyes off *her*. The ball's tight in her grip with a radiant smile on her face. Kemen's laughter carries across the field, and I smile.

"Emmitt, don't do it." He blocks my view and I push him aside.

"Don't you have a team to oversee?" I ask him.

"Nope." He slaps a football against my stomach.

That gets my attention. "Why?"

"Because practice is over." Kamal announces, noticing the pair at the end of the field. "Those two are having a good time. Is he one of ours?"

I glance around, and Coach Trent joins our little huddle.

"Yeah, don't you recognize his mother?" Dean crosses his arms over his chest.

"Ohhhh…." Kamal's eyes widen with his finger pointing at Amber with recognition. "The skirt."

"The skirt," Dean confirms. "I think the player has lost his touch."

"Like hell I have."

"You sure about that?" Kamal makes a move for the football, and I slip out of his reach.

"Don't sleep on me, baby. Ain't shit change but the date." I toss the ball. "Come on, Old Man Kamal.

You've been sitting behind that desk, eating chicken and waffles. You ain't ready for the kid."

"Always been a loud mouth."

I laugh as he sends the football soaring through the air. My body moves based on years of training, and without a second thought, I run long, catching it a few feet from Kemen and Amber. I flip the skin in the air, turning to the two people that have occupied my thoughts for most practice.

"Kemen."

"Coach E," he jogs over.

"Warm him up." I call to the guys. Dean and Kamal move like the pros they are. I throw Kemen the ball. "Toss a few and warm up your shoulder, and I'll take you through some drills. I need to holler at your mom."

Kemen looks over at Amber. I watch them communicate without a word. He's standing with his back straight, the ball tucked in his side, face tight as if waiting for her permission.

"Fine. Warm up. You still have homework."

"Yes, ma'am." He turns to leave. "Thank you, Coach E."

Kemen runs off leaving us alone.

"Homework? He's in summer school?"

"No, he's attending a software engineering camp at TSU for college credits."

"At thirteen?"

"Yes, at thirteen."

"That's impressive." I look over at the kid from a different perspective.

"Look, Coach Emmitt…" Amber sits forward, dusting the grass off of her hands. And I'm ready for more of her sass and attitude. "I apologize for earlier. It's been a long week. But I need to know, what's it going to take to get my son on that field?"

CHAPTER 7

AFTER OUR LITTLE FACE OFF, I stormed off in one direction and Emmitt went the other. The man annoys me and turns me on. He wears shades and yet I feel his eyes all over my body. All while sitting in the middle of the Emmitt Booker Fan Club.

When Chanel said the kids didn't come to play, *bay-bay,* she was speaking the god's honest truth. These mammas—whether they have a man or not—are down for whatever Emmitt's offering. And his ass stands in the middle, cheesing and smiling. Crossing those big arms over that broad chest and…

"What's wrong with you?" Chanel asked the second I dropped to the bleachers, ignoring the questioning stares of the others.

"I'm tired, and he just rubs me the wrong way."

"Girl, you better stop tripping. You need that scholarship. *Need*." Chanel shifted from the third bench to sit beside me. "So, whatever's annoying you, fix it because, news flash, Scarlette doesn't like you."

"What does that have to do with anything?"

"Scarlette's spoiled and petty, and she's not above giving the funds to another kid to fuck with you. Don't give her a reason to skip Kemen."

I shook my head. "I wish she would."

"Amber, you know I got your back, but you're wrong here. This is a major opportunity for Kemen, and you know he loves Emmitt."

"So, this is my fault?"

"Yes. Yes, it is. You know the power of our boys on the field together is undeniable. This is a chance for Brandon too. So, quit fucking us all and fuck Emmitt instead."

I almost broke my neck, turning to stare at Chanel. The Texas heat must have fried her damn brain. "What is wrong with you?"

"You! Get it over with and get that shit out of your system so we can get back to business." She hissed and her face twisted up like an old, nasty snake. "You're stomping around here with an attitude and it's not cute. I've offered to take a late lunch and—"

"No, Kemen isn't your responsibility."

"He's done everything you've asked him to do. Suck that shit up and fix this, Amber. Fix it. Here comes

Kemen." Chanel shifted back to the third bench, and I stood to meet Kemen, not expecting more of the same.

"Ma, you gotta chill." Kemen took off in a jog, and once again, I stormed off, this time behind my pissed son.

"What? He's taking it out on you like you drive yourself."

Kemen huffs and runs off. I stop following him and look down at myself then head to my car. My gym bag stays in my trunk. I'm petty, but not blind. The common denominator is me.

I opened the trunk of my car and push the miscellaneous clothing samples around in search of my bag. I don't have time to change clothes, so I'll have to run in my work clothes. I yank open my gym bag as if it's the cause of my frustration.

Life is on ten. I removed my dress shoes and slipped into my sneakers. *When did today become shit-on-Amber day?*

The sun beamed directly in my eyes as I searched the field for my son. Then I saw him running around the far end of the field. I walked to the edge and waited for him to reach me.

Today, I could use a drink and some silence. But everyone and everything is tap-dancing on my last nerve. My job is tripping about me leaving early to pick up Kemen. Nate is pissed because I won't fuck him. The one bright spot is the admissions counselor at Jordan Prep gave me until a month before school starts to find the money or she'll have to give Kemen's seat to another student.

This is when I'd rather lose myself in some good dick or chocolate. Not in that order. The weight and responsibility of wanting the best for my child is heavy as fuck and complaining about it won't add dollars to my bank account or get me any closer to getting my kid in that school. And screwing Coach Emmitt won't either. *But it would relieve the stress…*

I shake that thought from my head. Adding a new man to this hot mess would only add to my stress, and Nate used to be on speed-dial when I needed my itch scratched, but his ass was getting too clingy and now, with him refusing to help with Kemen's tuition, I'm putting a stop to his late night visits. Why he thinks I'd want a relationship with him is beyond me, especially when he's repeatedly shown I can't rely on him, not even when it comes to Kemen. And now he's avoiding my calls mad because I cut him off.

I have six weeks to magically find seventeen thousand dollars. This doesn't include uniforms or sports fees or bills.

Chanel's right. Kemen getting that scholarship would solve everything. And I'm not kissing Scarlette's ass, but I can stay away from her man.

Scarlette has stood on the sidelines and her desire to keep the mothers away from Coach Emmitt borders on hysterical. That woman growls every time someone even speaks to him. And like a man, he's clueless. That's a one-sided infatuation but ask me who gives a damn?

Not I.

I don't have the luxury of giving a damn. But I'll have to go through her to get my son that scholarship.

I jogged to catch up with Kemen. The second I settle into his easy pace, he leveled with me.

"Ma, what's the point of getting me on the team if you're going to get me kicked off?" I ran a little faster to see his profile. "I only see one solution. I'll get what I can for the next few days and don't participate in tryouts."

"What?"

"You think I don't notice you working through the night? Waking up early, taking on extra stores for more hours? This is how I can help us. I get good grades and I leave everything on the field. But I can't drive, and I won't get that scholarship if I can't get here on time. So, either we're all in or we're not."

Kemen's asking me to do better when I feel like I'm stretched to capacity. Frustrated because Nate gets to parlay around the country while I sweat it out on my own raising our son. Then he'll pop up at the end of the season like he did something.

However, this isn't about Nate or Emmitt or Scarlette. This is about my son. My little boy that's becoming a young man. And I'm proud of the man he's becoming.

"I'll fix it."

He slows to my pace, and we run a few laps before he talks again. "Did you know they are billionaires?"

"Billionaires? Who?"

"Those three." Kemen tips his head as we run past Emmitt, Dean, and Kamal.

"How do you know?"

"Mamma, you bitch and think I don't hear you? I listen to everything you say."

"Well, how about you listen to me and clean up your mouth?"

He laughs. "After you just threw a tantrum with Coach Emmitt?"

"Boy, keep playing with me and I won't feed you."

"But I do the cooking." He looks down at me with humor in his eyes.

People see us and think I give him too many liberties. But I found myself raising a little boy with no experience or perspective. All I knew was Nate and the knuckleheaded men around my old hood. Not all bad, and not all good, but none have the qualities I wanted for my son.

I want Kemen to be a man—honest, respectful, and

a gentleman. I want him to think for himself. To stand toe-to-toe with anyone and not back down. I don't want him scrapping to get by and I don't want him to settle when he deserves the world.

I had to change the way I parent. He knows I'm the parent, but I'm not above apologizing and admitting I'm wrong. It's the only way I could lead him into a life I know nothing about. Because I want him to be all the things I'm not.

So now we extend grace when we hit a bump in the road, and we talk about everything, knowing I've never done this before and neither has he.

We're in this thing together. Just the two of us.

"I really hate when you're right. Tell me about these billionaires."

"They have a business. Two of the three earned their first millions thanks to football. The rest came from their investments. I figure all we need is five million."

"What? We? Five million? What are you talking about?"

"I want to start a gaming company. I got a few kids at the school working on a prototype and I'm designing the app."

"What?" I stop and fold over, resting my hands on my knees.

"Football's our entry point, Ma." He stretches and I look up at him. "My plan is to finish high school with enough college credits to enter college as a sophomore. I'll play ball and get picked up by the NFL. My signing bonus will set us up for life."

"When did you come to all of this?"

"I told you, I got you."

We sit on the grass and I'm still shocked. When did it happen? My kid is becoming a man right before my eyes.

"Your sacrifice is driving me around. My sacrifice is staying at the top of my class and the best on the field. But this is only temporary."

Pride fills my chest. "I see you, kid."

"Damn right," his little cocky ass says.

I elbow him. "Keep playing with me and imma bust your ass." We laugh, both watching the game on the field. "Then why are you fighting me about the private school? Wouldn't that increase your chances?"

"It would, but academics is harder. It will take more to stay at the top, but it would land me in a better college. So…" He shrugs.

"Then I did something right?" I stand up, grabbing a football and toss it to him.

"Yeah, you did something right."

We tossed the ball round when we see Emmitt sprinting down the field in our direction. The football spins and he catches it with ease.

"Those are million-dollar hands. He came from right here. If he can do it, I can do it."

"Damn right."

"But it means nothing if I don't get on that field." He rests his hands on his hips. "That's my plan. Are we all in or all out?"

"I got you, baby. You don't have a better wing man than me."

Now, I'm sitting with Emmitt. He's clearly shocked by my apology. Juggling means I don't have time to dwell on missteps. I have to eat crow sometimes, tell me a person who hasn't. The key is not dropping the ball. The scholarship isn't guaranteed, and until they call Kemen's name, I have a major debt hanging over my head.

"Coach Emmitt, I want my son to excel in his academics and he wants to learn from you. I'm willing to do whatever it takes."

His eyebrows raise.

"Not that."

He laughs. "You're really no fun."

"I ran this field in dress clothes after working ten hours on my feet. I have no time for fun."

"You should." His eyes soften and the fairies in my stomach wake.

"You're stalling."

"No… I think I'm flirting."

"You think?" I mock offense just to hear him laugh. "You must hang with some basic-ass women."

"Oh damn, shots fired. Man down. Ain't nothing basic about me, baby."

"We need options…." I change the subject to keep from staring into his eyes. "Can you extend his grace period? He could run extra drills after practice."

"I can't coach him if he's late. I'm a man of my word and his teammates look up to him."

"And I can't get from the north side to the south side in 30 minutes."

"We have to find another solution. This is a lesson you want your son to learn. All he has is his word. We, as Black men, don't always get a second chance. We have to shoot our shot and make it count."

"I'll work it out." I lean back on my hands. My options seem slim, maybe I'll talk to my boss again.

"What if I could find you a job closer? Would that help?"

"You'd do that?" His offer surprises me.

"Yes. I want Kemen on my field as much as he wants to be there. He's a natural, and he has a lot of potential."

"So, what's this job?"

"Do you dance?"

"What kind of shady proposal—"

Emmitt holds up his hands. "I have some girls interested in majorette dance. They're mostly sitting on the bleacher waiting for the team to finish practice."

Yeah, because their mammas are hanging around, trying to catch a glimpse of Coach Emmitt. But I keep that thought to myself. "I could have two left feet."

"Thank God you don't," he says with such confidence that I turn my body towards him, curious about what he'll say next.

"How do you know?"

"The way you walk. I hear the tune playing in your head. It's the sway of your hips. The cadence of your steps. And those thighs…"

"What about my thighs?" I shouldn't entertain this conversation. But it confirms every tingle of awareness. "You've been staring at me the whole time."

"Let me take you out."

"Not happening, and ruin your fan club." I shake my head, chuckling. "I wouldn't want to ruin your reputation."

"My fan club?"

"Don't act like you haven't seen the titties and ass cheeks for days."

He barks a laugh, head back and it echoes around

us. I swear joy leaps in my soul. I shouldn't allow myself to be attracted to this man. It is impossible to ignore his captivating eyes, desirable body, and magnetic smile— everything stops when that smile spreads across his face and the sparkle of humor fills his eyes.

But hands down, all women on deck, *girl-you-wouldn't-believe-me*-but-it's-true moment happens when he laughs. Emmitt laughs with his whole body, it's loud and slightly jarring. He laughs often with no discrimination, and everyone is fair game when he cracks jokes. To me, it shows he doesn't take himself too seriously. I've never found humor as the most attractive feature in a man, but Emmitt seems to be so far out of my norm.

He stares at me as if he can read my mind. "I sort of think it's dope that you keep telling me no."

"Really?"

The jokester disappears and a fierce gaze of determination stares at me. This is when I should get up. I should excuse myself because I definitely don't have time or the bandwidth or the tools to deal with a man like him. I know my limits, even though this attraction appears to be mutual. But Emmitt isn't the kind of man a woman forgets.

Yet, against my better judgement, I extend my hand because I promised I'd fix my fuck up. I'd get my son on that field and if it takes shaking my ass on the sidelines to do it, well damn, I've done worse.

"Put my son on the field. And I'll handle the girls."

"You can't be late."

"I won't be late Coach Emmitt because I won't disappoint my son."

"It means that much to you."

"Yes." I stare him in the eyes. "He means everything to me."

Emmitt's gaze is so intense. I feel exposed, and when it comes to my son, I don't care that he sees my vulnerability, my fears, or my willingness to do anything for my kid. Because he's the absolute best part of me. And I gave Kemen my word.

"It's done. You have one week to prove to me you can get him here on time. Then we'll hire you for the rest of camp."

"I accept."

Emmitt takes my hand in his. That moment—the one where the world stops, and I can't breathe, and I can't look away—is happening *right now*. I try to pull away, but the damage is done.

The heat of his skin crawls up my arm. That deadly smile of his crosses his face and my hot pocket warms, and my breasts ache. I am asking for trouble because I know I want this man and I just agreed to work with him.

"And dinner?"

"No, Coach Emmitt. Because if I say yes—"

"When you say yes…" He coaxes.

Kemen waves his arms in the air to get my attention from across the field. I stand and dust the grass off my skirt. "Coach, *when* I say yes, it will be because I want to. What time do you need me to show up tomorrow?"

"Same time. I'll ask Chanel to notify the parents."

I nod. "I'll be here."

We talk for a few minutes, discussing my salary. It makes up for the extra hours and will save me on time. I accept for the second time. "I gotta go. We need to find something to eat and get home so Kemen can finish his homework. Thanks again."

I turn to leave, and he calls out. "Do you?"

I walk backwards to face him. "Do I what?"

"Want to have dinner with me?"

"That's for me to know and you to find out. Good night, Coach Emmitt."

"Then meet me tonight. Q's Spot." He stands in all of his finest.

I stop, almost stumbling over my feet.

"I'll be there around ten."

"For such a stickler regarding your time, you're not much of a rule follower."

"Not when it comes to something I want."

I'm surprised by his insistence and that I'm considering his offer. I mean, damn, the man stares at me, and I forget he's my son's coach and Scarlette might have it out for me. I glance back at Kemen, and he's occupied with Coach Dean. When I turn back, Emmitt's in front of me.

"This has nothing to do with my son."

"No. He'll earn his space on my field like the others. But when it comes to you…" He traces my body with his steamy eyes and I feel the heat pulsing through my veins. The man has only shaken my hand. I can only imagine how I'll feel when he touches me.

When…. Oh hell, not if. I take a step back, and Emmitt moves with me.

"Don't get scared on me now. If I remember correctly, you gave me some sound advice."

I chuckle. "But it wasn't an offer."

"Actually, you did, and I quote 'it don't get no better than this.' I'm a quality kind of man." He smiles in a matter-of-fact kind of way.

I had to open my damn mouth. But I meant that shit. I prop my hands on my hips. Emmitt drops his arms in front of his body, letting me get a good look at him up close. Even after spending the afternoon running up and down the field, he looks like a delicious chocolate treat. The cocky expression on his face challenges me, and I want to see if he can deliver.

"I don't have time for anything serious."

He moves closer. "Neither do I."

"My son comes first."

"As he should. It's something that makes you extremely attractive to me."

"Really?"

"Yes, the two of you..." He tilts his head back, as if searching for the right words. "You both intrigue me."

His admission has me ready to close the deal *now*. But my cookie is a gift. Now to see if he deserves it.

"Do you know what you're doing?" I point down at his cock, tilting my head to the side. "I'm not down with selfish lovers. No teeny weenies. No two-minute brothas."

Emmitt's laughter invades the night and I'm laughing with him, ready for his snappy come back.

"Damn. Now you're insulting my dick?"

I throw my hands up. "Nothing personal. Don't have me pulling out my good lingerie and my good sheets for a quickie."

"Your ass is crazy. But I got you, ma. Your place or mine?"

"But you didn't answer my question."

"And I won't." Emmitt gives me the quintessential *look at me* gesture. Then he extends his cellphone.

My heart slams in my chest, rattling my good sense. The innuendo hangs between us, and my pussy throbs in anticipation. The fact that he didn't answer nor is he offended says a lot. He's confident in his dick game.

The sexual tension mixed with his witty banter has

me more curious than cautious, even though I know we're playing with fire. He's still Kemen's coach, and Scarlette thinks she has him in the bag.

Am I really about to get this sexy ass man in my bed? *Hell, the fuck, yeah.*

I take the phone and his eyes buck.

"What? You thought I wasn't about to see if you're as smooth in the sheets as you are on the field?"

"Well, *goddamn*!"

"I have three caveats."

"I'm listening."

"Are you in a relationship?" He opens his mouth to respond, and I stop him. "I'm cool if you're a free agent. But I don't need some chick knocking on my door."

"I keep my situations drama free and I'm single. Next."

"What we do in my bed is between us?"

"No doubt. And number three…"

"You have to be honest with me. I'm young, but I'm not dumb. You probably got a woman in every town, and that's your business. I'm not expecting a ring or forever."

"What are you expecting?" Emmitt stares down into my eyes, stealing my breath.

"To get my back cracked, a few laughs, and to have a good time. No need to make it stressful. Life's stressful enough." We make plans to hang out tomorrow night.

I'll have the place to myself, thoughts about what I'll wear flutter through my mind. Then I look at the time, it's almost eight. "I need to go. Kemen has homework and I need to prepare for the dancers tomorrow. Here's your phone."

He takes it back with a chuckle. "You're a rare woman, Amber Evans."

"Yeah, I know. I'm a unicorn."

CHAPTER 8

I COULDN'T SLEEP. Emmitt had me in my bag last night. I can't remember the last time I flirted with a man, and it felt as natural as breathing. Then to give me the chance to share my first love: dance. And tonight, I plan to reward him with a sexy little number after I survive practice.

We jump out of the car, and I head to my trunk. I need to run inside and change clothes.

"Ma, you good?" Kemen grabs his bag.

"Yeah. What time is it?"

"We have thirty minutes, and you didn't have to pray the entire drive."

"Shut up. Let me get my speaker." I gather everything and slam the trunk closed. We hurry towards the center.

"Are you ready?" Kemen stands back, opening the door.

"Yeah," I whisper as we enter the building. "I'm a little nervous, I haven't danced in years." Then I pat my pockets, searching for my cellphone.

"Here. You left it in the car." He hands it to me.

"Thank you." I drop it in my gym bag. "Head in and I'll meet you here in five."

"Bet."

We part ways. I change clothes. Last night, I couldn't sleep with thoughts of Emmitt, and then I realized I needed a plan for today's rehearsal. I spent hours on YouTube watching dance stands. It took a few to get warmed up, then some of my old moves came back like it was yesterday. Dance was my life until I found boys. I wash my hands and throw my hair in a bun before meeting Kemen outside.

"You dance all the time," he picks up the conversation as we head out to the field.

"That's around the house. Today, I have to teach choreography and I'm rusty. Do you want to put your bag back in the trunk?"

Kemen throws his bag inside. We're early, and once his friends start rolling in, my kid circles back. "You got it. Let me know if you need me to bust a move for you."

He shakes around and I holler, laughing. "Scratch *that* idea."

"Don't sleep on me, Ma. You don't know the new moves."

"Boy, you stick to football, and I'll handle the dancing."

He chuckles and kisses my head. "Love you, Ma."

"Love you too. Be careful." The dangers of playing football never crossed my mind until Kemen started playing.

"Always. And, Ma…"

I drop my bag on the bleachers. "Yeah?"

"Thanks, I know you had to leave work early."

"I got you. Now show them how we do it." I wink and we bump fists. I watch him run to the field to warm up and I see we have an audience. Emmitt's on the field in his Hollywood shades. I acknowledge him with a slight tip of my head, and he passes a clipboard to Coach Trent, then walks my direction.

"Well… well… well…" He stops in front of me, crossing his arms. The beauty of the artwork on his arms shows in his sleeveless shirt.

"Surprised, coach?"

"A little."

"Good."

Emmitt looks edible, and knowing I'll have him in

my bed tonight makes me eager for the time to pass a little faster.

"What has you smiling like that?"

I glance around to ensure we're alone. "Knowing what I selected to wear for you tonight."

"I never took you for a tease."

I think about it for a second. "I'm not, but for you, I'll make an exception. How else will I keep your attention once the tits and ass crew rolls in?"

Emmitt's head falls back, and he laughs.

"I love when you do that." I admit before I have time to process why I disclose this fact. And under the heat of his direct gaze, I continue, "when you laugh."

He groans, and I wish I could see his eyes. But they're hidden behind those shades.

"Coach Emmitt, I'd like to see you in my office." Scarlette stands just over his shoulder.

"I'll let you get to work. I need to stretch before the girls get here." Sensation runs the length of my body. "I wish you didn't hide behind those shades."

"And I wish you had on more clothes. How do you expect me to focus with you wearing that?"

I look down at my outfit. I used to think I was too big to wear little crop top sets like this, then I realized when I look good, I feel invincible. "I think it's cute, plus it's hot."

"Hot as hell." Emmitt pushes his shades back, and

his eyes glow with lust. It's hotter than the Texas sun and I almost forget Scarlette's waiting for him.

"Coach." She steps closer.

Emmitt glances at his watch and back over at the field. "We have ten minutes before we huddle up. You'll have to catch me after practice. And you need to get the roster from Chanel, ah, here she is."

"Hey, sis," Chanel gives me a quick hug. "Coach. Scarlette."

An awkward tension hangs in the air.

"I need to warm up." I move to excuse myself.

"That's the problem. You can't work with the kids without a background check," Scarlette says.

"I have it right... here." Chanel retrieves a document from her folder.

"I didn't authorize this."

"Coach Emmitt had his team handle it."

"Oh." She takes the document.

Someone from DEK Ventures called me this morning, and we handled my employment paperwork. Scarlette doesn't look pleased.

"She's on our staff like the coaches. Anything else we'll have to cover after practice." He turns to walk away and stops. "Coach Amber, thank you for joining the team." Emmitt extends his hand, and I stare at it. This man ain't slick. Scarlette stomps off towards the center.

"Your ass is messy," I say for only him to hear.

Emmitt laughs. And I know I'm in trouble with this one. "I'm not messy. I just like things my way. Now, shake my hand."

I wag my head. "So you can zap me? No, thank you."

A smile curls his lips. "I think we're going to have a good time tonight."

Chanel gasps and I give Emmitt a *thanks* look. He shrugs. "My bad."

"I see how you want to do this, Coach Emmitt. Remember, I warned you." I take his hand and the chemistry between us is stronger than before. Our gazes lock and a wave of awareness throbs through my body. I quickly slip my hand from his.

"Coach E, they're ready," Coach Trent calls out.

"I'll be right there." He lowers his shades over his eyes. "I'll see you after practice."

I watch him walk away. "I bet his ass looks good in those football pants."

"Girl, what's going on tonight?" Chanel huffs. "Y'all got a date?" Her finger bounces between me and the man on the field.

"Not a date."

"What?" She stands in front of me. "Did your *fast* ass take my advice?"

"Maybe."

I walk back to the bleachers and remove my wireless speaker. Knowing Emmitt likes my outfit gives me an idea. I look over. Coach Kamal's on the field with the boys and Emmitt's standing on the sideline.

"You ready?" Chanel stands beside me. "I'll introduce you and you can begin practice. I created a welcome packet for the mothers. Review it and let me know if I need to change anything."

She gives me a copy. "Come through, sis."

"Well, you know." She takes a bow, and we start practice.

I have sixteen dancers ranging from age four to eleven.

"How many of you have danced with a team before?" A few hands go up.

"How many of you have never danced before?" A few look from side to side. "Don't be shy, we're a team here." A couple raise their hands.

"You're fine. Chanel, will you help me?" She jumps at the chance. "Let's set up over there."

We move to the open spaces at the end of the bleachers and start with stretching. I demonstrate and then I use Chanel as a model to show them form.

"Warming up and stretching is sometimes boring, but it's important. So, extend your arms like this and make sure you're not touching the girls around you."

The girls giggle and spread out. Chanel and I move

around placing girls in windows. When I have them where I want them, I stand in front. I glance back to the field, certain Emmitt's eyes are on me. Then I lose myself in the moment.

I wanted to become a career dancer. My mother couldn't afford formal dance lessons. Bootlegged cable taught me. I spent hours watching music videos. Mirrors and grass. Mirrors to perfect my form and grass as my dance floor. Because music never cared that I was a chunky girl, that my thighs rubbed together, that my stomach was soft. And with every move, I learned to love myself.

"You still got it, girl." Chanel tells me the second I drop to the bleachers. Most of the kids are gone, and I dismissed the girls until Monday.

"Thanks. The girls did good, didn't they?"

"Especially for the first practice. I need to see if we can get you in the gym."

"I like the sound of that." The thought of separating the younger girls from the older few would make teaching them easier. "You think Scarlette would go for it?"

"Probably not, but I have the keys. Girl, do you see what I see?"

I follow her gaze. There's a collective gasp as Emmitt removes his shirt.

"That's a damn sin…"

I don't know who said it but she's right. It is a sin to look like that, and when he points at me, I feel heat rush to my face. The women around me *ooohhhh* and *aaahhhh*. I don't blame them.

The coaches run drills for next week's tryouts. Emmitt is sculpted perfection, chiseled out of rich mahogany wood. The definition of his body is sickening, and for a second, I consider the state of my body. I've always been a big girl. My mother's death made me realize I had to take care of my health, and I do, but I'm still soft. Which I love but I'm an acquired taste.

"All I know is your ass better tell me everything," Chanel says. "When did all of this happen?"

"Let's go over there and grab my stuff." We change bleachers and I pack everything up for the night. "Last night."

"Is it a date?"

I shake my head.

"*Biiiiitch*!" She wiggles on the bench, slapping my arm. "You took my advice!"

"Yell it. Please. The whole world needs to know my business." I look side to side and lean in. "And yes. Well, not really. It sort of happened."

"How? Cause all I get is Lawrence's broke-

Whataburger ass."

"Whataburger?"

"That fool asked me out the other night." Chanel smacks her lips.

I sit, preparing myself for the drama, allowing myself to watch Emmitt on the field.

Then she continues, "Said fool proceeds to order everything on the menu. And we all know Whataburger ain't cheap. I'm thinking he must be starved after sitting at home playing video games all day. But whatever." Her dismissive hand says one thing and her hard eyeball says another. "Then we get to the window."

"He didn't have his wallet."

She pops up, throwing her arms in a touchdown motion. Then she spins back around with a look of horror on her face.

"What the fuck to I look like? Chase. PayPal. EBT. Hell, I don't know." Everyone's laughing and she's getting more pissed by the second. "He asked me out. I had to go pick him up and drop him off."

"He's lame. Why do you even bother?" I cover my mouth, trying not to laugh in my girl's face. This is why I don't date. I would have been the fool in the drive thru because that shit's foul. "Wait, did you pay for it?"

"Hell, to the *no!*"

Now, I'm dying. Leave it to her to get louder with

each sentence. We're all getting entertained by Chanel's love life.

"I told the young lady at the window all I wanted was *my* burger, *my* fries, and *my* shake. I paid and took his ass home." She huffs. "I'm done with him, for real this time."

She and Lawrence have one of these epic show-downs every couple of months. But Chanel doesn't like being alone, and after a couple of weeks payday hits, and he's back. I hope she means it this time.

"So, Coach E asked you, or you asked him?"

I think back on our conversation. "We sort of asked each other."

"He's definitely an upgrade."

"No, he's entertainment to de-stress and I'll get back to business."

Chanel stares at the field. "Yeah, right."

"I'm serious. And keep your mouth closed. I don't need my business getting back to your cousin."

"My lips are sealed. So, Kemen's staying at my house tonight?"

"Yeah, do you mind?"

"Nah, I got you." Her voice trails off and she waves.

"What's that about?"

"Nothing." She turns, facing me.

"No, I saw that little flirty wave. Who was it?" I scan the field. Coach Dean and Coach Kamal are married. "One of those college students?" I ask, shocked.

"No! Coach Trent."

"Coach Trent?" I use my hand to shield my eyes from the sun. Then I give him a good once over. This is the second week of the clinic. I've had a few conversations with him. And for all the years I've known Chanel, he doesn't compare to any of her previous boyfriends. That could be a good sign. "Is he even your type?"

"No. But he's nice, and he asked me out." She pauses and I'm sure we're thinking the same thing, but I'll let her be the one to bring it up.

"What did you say?"

"Nothing yet. I've never gone out with a White guy before."

"What's there to consider? A man is a man. He seems like a good guy."

"He is."

"He has a job. He's good with kids. He has a job."

"You said that already, heifa." We laugh. "You don't think it's like turning my back on Black Love?"

"No. I think it's about finding the kind of love that loves you back. I've had Black love, broke love, sorry-ass love, and now that I think about it, none of it was probably love. That's why it didn't last." I shrug and stare at the field. "I say try it."

The men head in our direction. Sweat trails down Emmitt's body, and I'm ready to take my own advice. I stand and meet him.

"I never took you for a tease," I throw his words back at him.

"Just a preview."

"Well, I like what I see."

"Oh, there's so much more." His words drip with promise, and I'm ready to take him home. *Now*. "You cooking tonight?"

My mouth drops open, and Chanel's ass starts coughing. Emmitt removes a towel from his bag and stares between us.

"I hope you got a strong stomach," Chanel mumbles and I stare at my best friend. "What? Girl, you know you can't cook. I can't let you go out like that."

I'm so embarrassed and Emmitt reads it on my face. "Don't worry about it. I'll pick us up something. Steaks sound good?"

I nod.

"How do I get Whataburger and you get steaks?" Chanel asks.

And in true Emmitt style, he's rolling. But Chanel is serious. So serious that she doesn't see Coach Trent approach the huddle.

"That's because you're dating the wrong man."

Chanel's mouth snaps closed.

"Women think too much except where it counts," Emmitt adds.

"What do you mean by that?" I ask.

"Most men show you exactly who they are, it's your choice to believe it or not. I bet he's never reached for his wallet first," Emmitt says.

Chanel wags her head.

"Why would he offer if he knows you'll pay for it?" Emmitt gives his infamous pose, with his arms crossed, looking over at Chanel.

"Because he's a man." I chime in, pissed by proxy.

Emmitt chuckles, turning back to Chanel. "Has he displayed any behaviors that you'd attribute to manhood?"

Her mouth falls open.

"This is where it counts. Does he have a job? A car? A bank account?"

Chanel shakes her head.

"Yo, E. You about ready?" Coach Kamal joins the huddle.

"Not yet." He pulls a shirt over his head. "Would you like a little advice?"

Chanel nods. Her jaw is tight, but I can tell she's listening to him. And she's not the only one. Emmitt's raining down the truth.

"In the words of my boy," he tips his head towards

Coach Kamal, "when a man shows you who he is, put that shit in ink. He has no incentive to grow up."

"School is in session." Coach Dean chuckles.

"What about you? I'm sure you have women in every state," Chanel says.

"I might. But I'm up front with my shit. They want to roll. Bet. They can't hang. I wish them the best. But when a woman's with me, she's treated like a lady. She'll never have to reach in her purse to pay for a damn thing. And it's not about the money. It's about respect."

"I'll pick you up tomorrow at seven."

"All right now, Coach Trent, shoot your shot," Emmitt encourages him.

"Brandon can hang with us for movie night." I add, giving her a little nudge in the right direction.

"You're a queen. Any man that doesn't recognize it doesn't deserve your time," Emmitt adds, and his eyes slide in my direction.

"All right." Chanel agrees, and we step away to give them some privacy.

"What time should I show up?" Emmitt asks.

"Whenever, I'm kid free until tomorrow at noon."

"Bet. I'll be there by eight. How do you like your steak?"

"You don't have to buy dinner. It's not like we're going on a date." The nonstop running of my thoughts last night helped me realize the importance of setting my expectations. No getting starry eyed or falling in love. This is purely about mutual attraction.

Emmitt gives me one of his stares.

"You don't have to give me a speech. I respect myself. But I'm also not letting this become more than what it is."

He leans back, crossing his arms. "So, you're not down with a quickie but you're cool with booty calls?"

"What are you trying to say?"

"I'm not saying anything. I'm trying to see where your head's at."

"Yeah, I'm cool with booty calls when I don't want to be bothered, when the expectations are clear."

"And tonight?" He drags his tongue across his bottom lip.

"I want to be bothered."

"Good. I need you to have a good meal because I'm not leaving until I get my fill." We laugh. "So, I'll ask again, how do you like your steak?"

The rest of the goodbyes floated around me. I rush home to shower and change, but the conversation weighs on my mind.

Emmitt's advice to Chanel reminds me of Nate. If I had to judge by his actions, we should have been over years ago. He's always thought about himself first and I don't see that changing. Maybe it's time to think about what *I* deserve.

CHAPTER 9

"Emmitt?"

"Look, Scarlette. I have plans and it's been a long week." I toss my stuff in the back seat before turning around. Scarlette's standing at the back of my SUV.

"The kids are having a great time. Parents are asking if you'll continue through the school year."

"Is this why you stopped me? If so, we can talk about this Monday." I close the door.

"No, I think we got off on the wrong foot. I thought we had a great time during your last visit. I'm just asking for a chance to see if the spark we had was real."

I shake my head. This is that shit Kamal warns me about. I always pick the woman with cotton in her ears.

"All I'm asking for is drinks. Drinks and conversation." She smiles and I think about the next six weeks.

"I'll think about it. Look, I gotta go." I open my door. "Is that your car?"

She nods.

"Head over and I'll wait for you to get inside."

Scarlette takes her time walking to the luxury sedan. "Thank you, Emmitt."

"No problem."

I wait for her to drive off and scan the parking lot to ensure everyone's gone for the weekend. Then I head to the hotel with Amber on my mind. But I need to decide how to handle Scarlette. Ignoring her is impossible and brushing her off will make the next six weeks miserable.

An hour later, I'm standing on a small joint porch ringing Amber's doorbell. The weight of my week rolls through my mind as I check out the street. I haven't been in this part of Houston in years. The street is quiet, and I see Amber's car in the driveway.

I reach to ring the doorbell again when the door opens. And she's standing with a lavender bustier with a matching silk robe.

I throw up a hand sending the driver back to the hotel and I open the screen door. Amber takes a small step back, enough for me to close the door behind us.

She takes my overnight bag and drops it beside the door. I trace a finger over the lace concealing her breasts.

"I'm starving," I admit. But it's not food I want.

I move the fabric aside and cup her breast, massaging it, rolling the peak of her nipple between my fingers. Amber's head falls back, and I drag my tongue up her neck. Kissing the pulse of her racing heart. Journeying to her pierced earlobe and her moans send heat through my body.

"Your lips are absolutely sinful. Do you know that?" I ask not waiting for an answer. I kiss her, taking my time, biting on her bottom lip, sucking on her top. She moans, pressing her body against mine and it's all the encouragement I need to explore her beautiful body.

Her tongue carves the part between my lips and her hot little hands wiggle down the front of my shorts. She caresses the length of my dick.

"Damn," she purrs.

I chuckle as my hands contour her breasts, riding the wave of her hips until my fingertips dig into the flesh of her bare ass. I lift her, pressing her back against the wall and she gasps. Her amber eyes round in shock.

"You had your caveats. Tell me how you like it." I suckle on her neck inhaling the fresh scent of citrus on her skin.

"I'm flexible." Her thick legs tighten around my

waist, and she starts a slow grind. "I'm not down with anal but I give good head."

"Fuck."

The next chuckle comes from her.

"Doggy style. Frog. Reverse cowgirl. Sixty-nine. I got you." I'm cataloguing every word. The sound of her raspy tone heavy with need has my dick rock-hard and I'm ready to dive deep inside her. "But I'll kick your ass out if I don't cum."

"I got *you*." I pull back staring into her beautiful eyes. "Which way is your bedroom?"

She points down the hall. "I can walk."

"I'm not ready to let you go."

Amber wraps her hands around my neck. Her kiss demanding, and I relax into the softness of her body following the sound of music.

"This it?" I mumble across her lips, and she nods. With one arm securely around her waist, I open the door. Candles light the room with nineties R&B playing. I lower her to the floor, taking in the space around me.

"I can blow them out if they're too much."

I slowly turn and I'm touched by her thoughtfulness. The visual of her gorgeous body in lingerie. My eyes travel from the top of her bun, the studs in her ears, the light makeup on her face, the cherry-red lipstick on her lips.

"I've had a *really* long week. Make me forget."

"Take off the robe."

Amber rolls her shoulders never dropping her gaze and the fabric flutters to the carpet in a pool of silk.

"Turn around." She moves to follow my command. "Slowly, Amber, I don't want to miss a thing." She rocks from foot to foot. Lace covers her breasts, and the patch of heaven between her thighs. When she's facing the bed, Amber glances back as I admire that ass. And when she makes her way back around, I notice the strappy heels and her lavender painted toes. I don't know where to begin. Then I reach for the hem of my shirt.

"Let me."

I nod. Not trusting myself to speak. She stalks across the room like a woman on a mission and it's sexy as fuck. Closing out my affairs in Dallas and flying back and forth between our projects around the country occupied my time for months. I was ready to find some action in Houston. Now, I'm glad I waited.

"You have an amazing body." Her hands crawl beneath my shirt. She tosses it to the floor. Her hand grips my waistband leading me to the bed.

I remove the box of condoms from my pocket seconds before she slides my shorts to the floor. Her gaze zeroes in on my dick.

"Can you handle it?" I tease, and she licks those luscious lips.

"You tell me." Amber takes my dick in her mouth and I'm the one shocked. The play between her tongue and her tension feels so fucking good I could bust right now.

"*Goddamn*…. Fuck." Then she drops to her knees. I hold the back of her head as she bobs, taking me deeper, driving my shit to the back of her throat.

I rip open the box, fumbling to remove the wrapper. "Ass up, Amber."

She sits back with a look of pleasure on her face. She wipes the moisture from the sides of her mouth sliding up to the edge of the bed. Then she reaches for her heels.

"Leave them."

I roll the condom down my cherry-coated brick watching her climb into the bed. I follow and tear the thin fabric of her thong panties, kissing both cheeks of her ass.

"Get a pillow, baby, it's about to get rocky." And I plunge in her tight pussy.

"Fuck…." She screams and I hold on to her hips. plowing so deep, we both groan in pleasure.

Her ass jiggles, bouncing off my body. The sounds of the music disappear, and I revel in her moans. The deeper I go, the more shit I talk, and she's begging for more.

"Is this what you wanted Amber?"

"Yeah… yes… *Fuck*."

She buckles and I know she's about to come. "You ready, baby?"

"Yes…"

"Yes, who?"

"Yes… Emmitt."

But Amber ain't no punk. She throws her ass back and her pussy grips my dick so tight, I fold over. I grab her shoulders making sure she can feel my shit in her throat.

"I bet you won't forget it. My name is all over your pussy."

She bucks, heaving, screaming to the heavens, and it's music to my ears. But I'm not letting her ride this ride alone. I hold her breasts in my hands and jackhammer into her until my nuts curl up, filling the latex with my seed.

I roar and we collapse. My eyes fall closed as we struggle to breathe.

"*Shiiitttt*… You need to patent that damn dick."

I look over at Amber and die laughing. "Your ass is a fucking fool."

~

"I CAN'T REMAIN in this bed without food." Emmitt climbs out of the bed, and he is a glorious sight. He heads to the bathroom, and I watch until he's out of sight.

We never had those steaks and my lavender bustier is ruined. I stretch knowing I'll be sore. That man asked for every trick in my sexy-times book and added a few more.

It's Saturday and I need to account for every second if I want to stay the course. I need to prep for the girls next week, visit a few boutiques, and grab some frozen pizzas for the boys tonight. Then there's laundry and I have to update the monthly reports for my boss.

"Do you mind if I check the frig?"

"I don't mind, but you might not find anything." I mumble, mentally drafting my grocery list. I roll over and Emmitt's naked in the doorway. My gaze covers his body, lingering over his cock. Just the sight of that dick makes my pussy pulse.

"Get that ass up. I need you energized for the next round."

"Next round?"

"I bet you won't talk that shit next time. Get a move on." He smacks my ass and I roll over drained. The kind that paints a goofy smile on my face. Then, I reach for my robe.

"No clothes." He tosses over his shoulder making a stop by the bathroom.

I freeze and heat burns my cheeks. For all of my confidence, I'm not a naked in the daytime kind of woman. I have stretch marks, dimples, and rolls. I'm not ashamed but I mask my imperfections with sexy lingerie.

"How can you possibly be shy after last night?"

"That was by candlelight, not sunlight."

His laughter echoes in the bathroom. I hear the toilet flush and the water running. "It's your house, and your body. But I can make no clothes fun."

"That's easy for you to say. Your body is perfect."

"I'm not perfection. My body is how I earn my living. When I take care of it, it takes care of me."

I sit up in the bed. "What's that like? I see Kemen running up and down that field and it still scares me to death. But he loves it."

"It's what I do." He shrugs, sitting at the foot of the bed. "And once I'm on the field, I'm locked in with my eyes on the end zone." He lifts a finger as if he got an idea. "I'll order food. What time is it?"

"Seven fifteen."

"Check out the menu." He tosses his phone and I scan it, picking a platter.

"Southern Soul delivers?"

"No, but I have a concierge membership." He

makes the call and I run to the bathroom to freshen up.

A concierge membership? Not Uber Eats or Favor but a concierge membership. I shrug, he won't hear me complain since I'm not the best cook. I'd rather he order food than me embarrass myself after such an amazing night.

I stare at my reflection in the mirror and the evidence of what we did last night. Passion marks adorn my skin and I'm relaxed down to my bones.

Emmitt loved on every inch of my body. Then I hear the wrapper tear.

My gaze meets his in the mirror and he stands behind me. His hands glide over my ass, run up my waist and down my arms. He places my hands on the counter, then positions my hips before filling me inch by inch. My head falls back, *Imma be bowlegged messing with this man.*

"Open those beautiful eyes, I want to see you."

I stare at him. This feels like a dream, the rhythm of him sliding in and out of my body. The sound of my wetness. He kisses across my shoulder, up my neck, and hovers over my ear.

"Thank you," he whispers before nibbling on my earlobe. "Are you available tonight?"

"No," I groan. The boys are with me tonight, and I can't do this two nights in a row.

"When?"

My eyes snap open seeking his. "I don't think that's a good idea."

"I *think* I can convince you otherwise." His free hand cups my heat and I fall back against his chest.

I buck, arching my back, begging him to go deeper. The constant pressure on my clit mounts and it feels humanly impossible to come again. He gave me more orgasms that I could count and, apparently, he's not done.

"You can't deny this."

"Why?"

"Because I want more of you. Name the time and the place, baby, and I'll be ready." His hypnotizing gaze holds me hostage. "Say yes, Amber."

And like magic, I'm spun around, watching his long, thick dick slide inside of me. Stretching me, molding me, ruining me for any other man. Emmitt guides his hands beneath me, bringing me to the edge of the counter, and pumps inside of me. The ache hurts so good, it's fast and demanding. The rhythm makes my titties bounce and I grip his shoulders fearful that I'll break, and I'm willing to give him whatever his chocolate ass wants.

Then the wall of my pussy quivers. Pleasure rips from my soul and I scream my surrender. "Yes!"

Emmitt cups my face and tongues me down. "Good girl."

CHAPTER 10

LIVING IN A HOTEL SUITE, no matter how luxurious it may be, never feels relaxing. My mind associates hotels with work. City to city. Football field to football field. Kamal and Jayda offered their guest house, but I don't want to intrude, and I value my privacy. Which leaves me alone tonight with too much time to think about last night—and this morning.

I sit back, trying to pinpoint the moment I lost control of this situation. The light on the muted television captures my attention until a flash of purple fabric takes me back to Amber.

Amber is… unexpected.

Maybe it was the lavender bustier, or her deep throating me, or the feel of her riding me. I could make a case for all of it, but even after having her every way imaginable, I want more.

However, the nature of my world centers on clear-cut boundaries. I chuckle. Damn, I'm sounding more and more like Kamal. Staying drama-free comes with rules and risks. But the risks make this little game of mine enticing and I'm a pro at getting what I want. And I want Amber.

My rules are simple.

Rule number one: I don't have sex where I lay my head. That means women aren't invited to my suite.

Rule number two: We're free agents. Except I don't fuck with women that have fucked with my boys or teammates. That's drama I can't afford. I have to trust my boys and the men protecting me on the field.

The final rule: Don't ask, don't tell. I don't need to know her body count, and she won't know mine. We strap up, ride the ride, and when it's over, we part ways, equally satisfied.

But Amber's nothing like Ebony or Scarlette, and as of yesterday, she's an employee and her son's one of my players. I stand, pacing the length of the living room. Asking each step to give me a plan, a plan that will get me back to her. My dick jumps at the thought.

"Just one more time…" I pick up my phone to send her a text and stop myself. "What the fuck did she do to me?"

I walk to the window overlooking the Houston skyline. The city is beautiful from here. You'd never know the grit and grind crawling through the streets. I rub a hand over my eyes, and when my phone rings, I welcome the distraction.

"Yo, what's up?"

"Hey, Emmitt."

"Robin?" I glance back at the screen. "What's up?"

"Huh… How are you?"

"Never better."

"Right." She exhales a shaky breath and I wait, not eager to make this conversation easy for her. "I… uh…. Tomorrow, I'm cooking dinner and I'd love to have you. It's nothing fancy but maybe we could eat and catch up."

"I have plans."

"Right, maybe next week. Pick the day and I'll fix whatever you like."

"I'll be busy then too." I stand up and grab my keys.

"Emmitt, please. I'm trying."

"Robin, you're about twenty years too late. Look, I'm about to bounce. Is there anything else?"

"No. I love you."

"Yeah, I bet you do." I disconnect the line, trying to outrun the pain of rejection.

~

DRINKS ON ME. Q's Spot @ 10. I add the brown fist bump to my text message in our group thread before climbing into my SUV. The chime of their responses settles the rage rushing through my veins. The tires squeal as I take the tight curbs of the parking garage faster than I should. The beauty of Texas is the highways, and I have a full tank of gas and a few hours to burn.

I lean forward with my hands curled tight around the steering wheel, keeping my eyes open, pushing the voices out of my head. My phone rings, announcing *Miss Jackie.*

I hit ignore, turning the SUV toward the highway. My phone rings again, *Miss Jackie.* I weave through traffic until I reach a clear patch. And I floor it. The surroundings pass in a blur. The Caddy responds happily, eating up the highway.

Miss Jackie. Miss Jackie. King Kamal, sounds through the speakers.

I chuckle, seething. "Yo, what's up?"

"You good, brother?" Kamal asks.

"Always."

"Where are you?" Dean asks.

"I-10. Guessing I'm halfway to San Antonio." I laugh, but the ache in my chest isn't funny.

"Bro, turn around and let's talk when you're not pushing a two-ton truck." Kamal suggests.

"How does she think I'm supposed to forget every-thing? Fuck her!"

"E… Been there. But what we don't need is your ass hauled off to jail for thinking the Escalade has wings," Dean says.

I jerk the SUV to the shoulder of the road and slam on the breaks. We hold the line, and I search for the right words to stop my head from spinning. I don't want to hate her. But no other word represents the level of animosity and rage I have for Robin Booker. Not a single one.

I jump out of the truck. My eyes burn with rage and my world's coated in red. I ball my fist and come down on the hood like the Hulk.

Once.

Twice.

… a third time I pound my frustration. I pull back and stop at the sound of Miss Jackie. "Emmitt, baby, please. Please."

My head drops, and I take a deep breath. *She's not worth it.* I climb back my truck.

"Y'all, I'm good. I'll be at Q's." I disconnect the line, then call the first person who comes to mind. Ready to get lost in her. Amber's phone rings until the voicemail plays. "I want to see you tonight." I fall back in the seat and exhale. "Make it happen, baby."

AN HOUR LATER, I roll up to Q's Spot. I enter and I'm greeted by a pop on the speakers and the hum of conversations. I ask for Q and he descends a staircase like *the man*. He's stopped by people everywhere he turns.

Q kisses cheeks, pounds fists. "Welcome, bro. What's good with you?" He pulls me in for a brotherly hug, then looks me in the eyes. "Looks like you could use a drink."

"Or two."

"I got you. Come on." Q guides me through the club. "VIP or bar?"

"Bar." I need the noise to quiet my thoughts. I can't lose my shit every time I talk with Robin. Something's got to change.

"Bet. Hang out right here. I'll get you set up." He turns to the bartender. "Take care of him. On the house."

"Man, you don't have to…"

"You're family. And you look like you need that shit." He chuckles.

"Thanks, man." I exhale.

"No problem. That's what family's for. Be right back."

I nod, order a fireball and toss the cinnamon

whiskey back, slamming the glass on the bar. "One more."

"Coach."

I glance over. "Scarlette."

"Mind if I join you?"

"Not at all," I say, needing a distraction.

Scarlette orders a glass of wine and sits on the barstool beside me. I down the second shot, welcoming the numbing effect of the alcohol.

"E, your table's ready." Q pats my back.

I stand and introduce them. "Quan Montgomery, Scarlette Knight."

We follow the waitress and I sit in the booth, not surprised when Scarlette sits across from me.

"Order you some food to eat up that liquor?" I nod and Q leans in. "Give me your keys."

I stare at his hand. "King Kamal?"

"Nah, Ma. You're on her shit list." I relinquish my truck keys. "And just a little brotherly advice, call her before she calls you." He slaps my back with a thud. "It was nice meeting you, Scarlette." He turns back to me. "Holler at me when you're ready to leave."

"Kamal and Dean should be here shortly."

"Cool, well, tonight's on me. Enjoy. Let me know if you need anything."

"Thanks, man."

Q smiles and disappears in the crowd.

"What a surprise seeing you here tonight."

I drop an arm over the back of the booth and wait for her to continue. The reality that I just fucked up a rental, hung up on Miss Jackie, and Amber hasn't returned my call has me in rare form. That I'd let Robin get under my skin shows a level of weakness I'm not proud of, but fuck, I'm human.

"How are you feeling about the progress of the clinic?" Scarlette tries again, taking a sip of her wine.

I appreciate her selecting a safe subject. And on the strength of her helping us launch this project, I decide not to be an asshole. "It's cool. But more challenging that I expected."

"In what ways?"

I think about her question. "Managing so many moving parts. The kids, the staff, the parents."

"Welcome to my world."

We share a laugh and I lean forward, resting my forearms on the table as the waitress approaches the table. We order and I send a quick text to the guys, letting them know I made it. Then I turn my attention to Scarlette.

"How are you feeling about the clinic?"

We talk and I push the day aside. This is the Scarlette I kicked it with last summer. We discuss the progress of the camp and her plans for future clinics featuring baseball, basketball, and track.

"What about programs for girls?" I ask, throwing back some fries.

"I will eventually, but we don't get as much participation. It's hard to justify the expenses. We have basketball and volleyball in our afterschool program though."

I nod, not agreeing, but it's her center. We eat through a platter of wings and drink beer. The DJs spinning and I'm feeling more like myself until I see someone across the room. The woman looks like Amber and she's chopping it up with a dude.

I pull out my phone and send her a text. *You down for some company tonight?*

A device on the woman's table glows and she stares down at it and turns it over. *Ain't that a bitch?* I stand, remembering Scarlette. "Do you want something from the bar?"

"We can order from the waitress." Scarlette's hand covers mine.

"I need to hit the bathroom. Be right back."

"Do you want me to order something?"

"A beer is cool." I call over my shoulder, moving towards the table. The dim lights make it hard to see. I slow down as I approach the table, and suddenly, I'm staring into Amber's golden eyes. Her mouth falls open.

Bathroom, now. I mouth, not stopping until I'm in the hallway outside the unisex bathroom. Buzzed thanks to the shots, I stand back, playing it cool, but

I'm losing my fucking mind. I should have kept my ass in Dallas. But it's too late. I spin in time to see a goddess in action. Her fucking jeans looking painted on those legs I had wrapped around my waist just this morning. She strolls with a mean mug on her face, and I meet her a second away from being pissed.

"What the fuck is your problem?"

I wrap my hands around her neck and kiss her. Not no soft shit, but my tongue is down her throat, invading her mouth, and she feels like air. Her hands grip my wrists. We're kissing and I want more than her mouth. I wrap my arms around her waist, lifting her from the ground, carrying her to the bathroom. The door closes behind us and I lock it.

"We can't do this."

"We're doing this. Ass up, Amber."

She stares at me, and I swear she sees through me. She takes a step, gathering my face in her hands. "What happened?"

"Nothing." I remove a condom from my pocket, tearing the package open with my teeth.

"You're not about to fuck me in a club bathroom. That's what you're not about to do."

"How quick you moved on."

"Fuck you, Emmitt. You need to leave that liquor alone."

"What you won't do, another woman will."

Her head snaps back. "Good night, Emmitt."

Amber turns to leave and I don't blame her, but I don't want her to leave. I reach for her, and she snatches away.

"Wait, I apologize."

"Lose my number and tell Scarlette I said hi." Amber storms out of the bathroom.

I remain unmoved until I hear a knock.

"Emmitt. Are you in there?" Kamal yells over the music.

I slowly open the door.

"Let's get out of here." Dean steps inside with a hand behind me.

I nod. I've done enough damage for the night.

"Uncle Emmitt.... Uncle Emmitt..."

My head pounds. "How many shots did I have?" I say to myself, looking around, and I'm not in my suite. This must be Kamal's guest house. I fall back and let sleep take me.

"Uncle Emmitt..." This time Reese sounds double. "Nana said it's lunchtime."

She holds out "time" like she's auditioning for American Idol. And my head can't take it.

"I'm coming. Tell her I'll be right there."

"Yes, sir."

The second it's silent, I roll over and try to go back to sleep. But the events from last night flash before my eyes and I realize I fucked up last night.

I reach for my phone to check the time, and it's almost one. *How'd I sleep the entire day?*

I dial Kamal with my face plastered to the bed, and before he says a word, I ask, "On a scale between one and ten, how mad is she?" Shame curls in my stomach and I can't blame anyone but myself.

"One is…"

"Upset."

"Ten is…"

"Enraged."

"Roughly… a thirteen point five."

I chuckle, glad my head stopped throbbing. "That's not on the scale."

"You hung up on her and you ignored her phone calls. That's some off-the-scale shit."

"Man, I know." I push up to a sitting position. "Remind me to never drink again."

"You got it. Come up to the house."

"Roger that."

I stand, and the sight of my reflection in the mirror startles me. Man, I had a rough night. I drag out of the guest house to talk with Miss Jackie and my next stop is to apologize to Amber.

"You need to move faster than that, old man. Practice starts in…" He glances down at his watch. "Two hours."

"What?"

"Yeah, you slept through Sunday. You'll have to smooth things over with Mother later. This is the first day of tryouts."

That wakes me up. "Damn, how many shots did I drink?"

"I don't know but you need to leave that liquor alone."

"Apparently. You got some clothes I can wear? I don't have time to go to the hotel."

"Yeah, I'll grab something for you to freshen up." Kamal passes me a plate of pancakes. "Let it absorb the rest of that *licka* out ya system."

"Man, shut up." I tease back, taking them. I eat them quickly and down two bottles of water.

"Here."

I take the clothes, and after I clean up, I consider calling Amber, but I need to talk to her in person.

CHAPTER 11

"I'M HAD MORE sex this weekend than…." I think over my life and I'm quite certain of my response. "*Ever*."

"Whhhaaaatttt…." Chanel sings.

"Girl, I feel like Jada off Jason's Lyric, all regal and loved and, girl, I can't explain it." I roll over on my back, staring at her ceiling. That man sweated out my hair and *everythang*. And when he finally left, the reality of our night sent me running next door to talk with my best friend.

Chanel is the one person I can tell anything, and there's no judgement. Her advice isn't always the best, but she's someone I can work through my problems, and something tells me Emmitt is a problem.

"He wants to do it again."

Chanel stops and stares at me. "And that's a problem?"

"Yes, it's a problem. First, he's Kemen's coach…"

"And… he was when he had your ass screaming through the walls last night." She sits on the end of the bed with the hundredth outfit crumbled in her lap.

"My bad."

"Girl, shit, at least someone's getting some good dick." Chanel holds up the olive-green jumpsuit. "I don't like this one either. What about this?"

I sit up ready to spill my guts, and it hits me, Chanel never asks me to pick her date outfits. "What's going on with you?"

She stands in the mirror holding another dress. "This ain't it either."

She's returns to the closet, and this time, I follow her.

"What's going on? And stop pulling these damn interview dresses." I take her hand, dragging her back to the bed. "What's up?"

"I'm tired of being burned."

"What do you mean?"

"Yesterday, Coach Emmitt was right. Lawrence is just like…"

"Todd."

She nods. "And Todd was like…"

I think back. "Andrew."

"See, I don't even remember their names. I pick the same man over and over…" Her shoulders slump.

"I think that's normal. We sort of pick what we know or based on our environment."

"But that's not what I want. A man expecting me to pay for his food, and his bills—"

"You been paying his bills?"

"No, but I loaned him some money."

"How's he supposed to pay you back? He doesn't have a job."

Chanel falls silent. This is how we work. We sort of balance each other out.

She went to college, I didn't. She earns decent money at the center, and I do okay, but I'm always barely getting by. Last year, we came together and bought this townhouse, and it was a game changer. It helped me stretch my finances. We enrolled the boys in a better school, and we moved away from our old neighborhood. And that move really showed me how much environment played into our decisions.

I doubt we would have considered giving up Nate and Lawrence if we were still living around the way.

"I think it's time for us to make another move." I look over at her. "Look at us. We're beautiful, young, and driven. We can do whatever we want with whomever we choose. So, let's chose different."

"I like the sound of that. New men, better careers, a summer refresh."

"Better careers?"

Chanel gathers my hands in hers. "Yes. Better careers. I know you love the boutique. But is it worth staying there if you have to stress over every financial decision? Either they need to pay you more or you need another job."

"I don't know but…"

"No buts, Amber. I'm next door now and Kemen's thirteen. He's mature enough to come home and handle his homework until you get off work. As for me…" She looks off and we're both lost in our thoughts.

Energy whirls in my body and I'm not sure whether it's fear or excitement. I've never given much thought to changing jobs. "But I love my job."

"Are you sure about that?" Chanel faces me. "I think you used to love it. When you moved from hourly worker into management, and you love the flexibility. But wouldn't you really love getting a new car and paying for Kemen's tuition without stressing? That's what more pay and a better position could afford you."

"I am tired of being broke. And begging Nate to help with Kemen's expenses. I'd like to confidently handle it on my own."

"You are handling it on your own. It's time for you to handle it and have money in the bank. Savings. Hell, a vacation. When's the last time you had a real vacation?"

"Never."

"Well, there you go. More money. A real vacation. And more dick."

I holler. "Who said anything about dick?"

"You don't expect us to get rid of the old dick and not get a new dick in its place."

"Please, stop saying—"

"Fine. I'll stop saying it, but you're glowing with the aftermath of great dick. And I want some. Not yours but my own, and help me find an outfit. I can't be late." She jumps up.

"What about you? What do you plan to do with your job?"

She stops and props a hand on her hip. "That's where I need your help."

"Me?"

"Yes, I want to use your dance program to show Scarlette she should make me program director. I get paid nicely but if I had some experience in development, I could stay or apply for positions with another center."

"You really like working with nonprofits."

"I do. But I'd like to have more scholarships and more programs for girls other than sports."

I sit, thinking about all we've said. "What would I do?"

"That's the beauty of this plan. You can do anything

you want. Go back to school. Start your own business. What about looking at similar positions with a larger store?" She stops in front of the mirror. "I think this is the one."

I stand up and look at her through the mirror. "You must be really nervous."

"How'd you guess?"

"Because you're about to wear your Sunday dress on Saturday." She gasps and I burst into laughter. We laugh until we cry. Then I enter her closet.

I walk the length of her closet, which mirrors mine, running my hands over the garments until I find the focal item. A cream romper. It has a flirty off-the-shoulders top. Now for the shoes....

I walk back and forth until I see the perfect sandals. "Are your toes polished?"

"Always."

I grab them and exit the closet. I lay the clothes on the bed and examine them. I need a wow factor. "Jewelry."

I spin around and pick through her collection when a medallion catches my eye. And then I lift it from the box, giddy. The layer necklace set is perfect. "Oh… she cute."

Chanel sits back, watching my every move. I'm in my zone. I snap my finger and return to her jewelry box. "Earrings and that chunky ring I got you for Christmas. Get your pink Chanel purse."

She runs off.

"That man knows who he's getting. Don't go as anything or anyone other than yourself." I assemble my vision on the bed. The romper, jewelry, the purse on one side, the shoes on the other. Then we stand back. "You need a pop of color. Grab your red lipsticks."

I pull out my phone to take a picture and notice a missed call from Emmitt. Just seeing his name makes my body tingle all over. I'll call him later when I'm alone.

Chanel returns with four options. I swatch each one on her arm before deciding. "This is the one."

"Oh bitch, you bad." Chanel snaps. "And this is it. This is what you do next."

I blink, not sure what she's talking about.

"This, Amber. This is what you do next. We find a way for you to get paid doing this."

I help her get dressed, and my mind is spinning. I buy clothes for a living, but I never considered... "What would you call this? Styling?"

"Yes, or personal shopping. How do I look?" Chanel fastens her shoe and stands in front of me.

"You look beautiful."

I take several pictures. I'm swiping through them when Chanel asks, "What will we talk about?"

"The man is White not an alien." I fluff her curls a little, I turn her to the mirror to see for herself. "Tonight, you'll get to talk with him alone. Get to know him outside the center."

"It just feels so different."

"You're overthinking. It's one date. Not forever."

"Uh-huh." She spins around. "I think you should take your own advice."

"What are you talking about?"

"Don't overthink this thing with Emmitt. He's here for the summer." She turns back to the mirror, smoothing the dress out. "I say let him wine and dine you. Fuck you into a glorified stupor. And when the summer's over, you can return to booty calls with Nate."

I elbow her. "I'm done with Nate. And Emmitt's great but…"

"But what? Don't let that man dick-matize you. You heard him yesterday, this is what he does. I say enjoy him. But a man like that ain't checking for women like us. Not long term. They pick models, get married, have little model kids, and always have a side chick. Emmitt is a fun thing, not a forever thing. Understand?"

I nod.

"Just have fun."

JUST HAVE FUN... Chanel left for her date with Coach Trent. The boys are fed and playing video games in Kemen's room. And I'm laying here thinking about Emmitt. He's leaving town in six weeks and it's not like I'm in the position to have a relationship. I'm in need of a miracle, and adding Emmitt to the mix seems like a recipe for a disaster.

I shove my face into my pillow and scream my frustration into the understanding cotton.

"You good, Ma?"

I toss the pillow aside. "Yes. No. I don't know."

Kemen walks in and lies on the bed beside me. I'm resting on my stomach and we both turn facing each other, resting our heads in our hands.

"You have company."

"Brandon isn't company. And he's on the phone."

"With who?"

"His girlfriend."

"Girlfriend?" I move to sit up and look down at Kemen. "Does his mother know?"

He falls back and tosses the pillow in the air and catches it. "I'm sure she does."

If Brandon has a girlfriend, then... "What about you?"

"Nah... And I'd tell you if I did, so stop stalling. What's up?"

I lay back down and tell him about my conversation with Chanel, minus the Emmitt part. One night doesn't feel significant enough to mention to him, and I'm not sure if he'll freak out since he looks up to Emmitt.

I grab my phone and nervously show him the pictures.

Kemen sits up, swiping through the pictures. "This is dope, Ma."

"Really?"

"Yeah. You need to start an Instagram account." He pulls out his phone and clicks around before turning it in my direction. "Like this."

I scroll through the feed. What am I doing? Am I really thinking about this?

"I think you should do it."

"I'll think about it. I can't do anything until the fall. I have enough on my plate."

"Not if you let me attend Yates."

"No, sir," I point at him. "Jordan Prep with no bitching. Remember?"

"Yes, ma'am. Do you mind if we go to the movies instead of hanging out around here?"

"That's cool. I'll drop you guys off."

"Bet."

He runs off and I look at my board. I've never considered starting my own thing. But Chanel's advice mixed with Kemen's goal of starting his own gaming company makes me wonder if it's time to step outside my norm. Maybe it's time I do something different.

I drop the boys off and give them until one. The movie theatre is in a metroplex where their friends like to hang out. This gives me a few hours to burn. I could go home but a celebratory drink sounds nice.

"Dinner and a drink." I think I can squeeze this outing into my budget. Q's Spot is a grown and sexy spot with bangin' food and the best DJs and it's close to the movie theatre.

Look at me. I had Emmitt on Friday and a dinner date with myself on Saturday. This is already different. I turn up my music and turn left instead of a right and I'm having a blast until I see Emmitt with Scarlette.

CHAPTER 12

I DON'T SEE Emmitt's Escalade. I waited for his call Saturday night. Then I expected to hear from him on Sunday. And in a stretch, I thought he'd at least text.

"You good, Ma?"

"Yes, what about you? Are you concerned about tryouts?"

"Nah, this is what I do. But I would like to warm up. Join me." Kemen opens the door and I do. I'm ready for a good run to clear my head.

I crouch down to retie my shoe and hear a car door slam.

"Hey, Coach."

"What's up, Young King? You ready for today?"

I have no desire to see Emmitt, but he doesn't sound like himself, and when I look over, he's talking with Kemen hidden behind his shades. Something happened Saturday, and we went from zero to one thousand in a nanosecond. To avoid him, I circle around my car and grab my stuff. And when I close the trunk, Emmitt's waiting.

"Amber, I apologize for my behavior Saturday night."

"For trying to fuck me in a bathroom or spazzing out on me?"

"Both."

"Remove the shades." I cross my arms over my chest, waiting for him to remove those damn shades.

"I look like shit."

"Tough."

Emmitt pushes the shades back and what lurks in the depths of his eyes grabs ahold of my soul.

"What happened?"

"Nothing, just too many shots." He lowers the glasses back over his eyes.

"That's your story? Too many shots?"

"Yes, Amber."

"Fine. Well, I don't accept." I head to the bleachers to drop off my bag and join Kemen on his run.

"What do you want me to say?"

"I want you to tell me the truth."

"There's nothing to tell."

I stop, and Emmitt anchors his hands on my shoulders to keep from stumbling into me. The moment he touches me, my heart races and my body aches. I have a choice. Pursue this or walk away. And there's no reason I should care one way or the other. I've only known the man for three weeks. Yes, we had amazing sex. But sex is sex.

"I don't have time for this. Apology accepted." I jog off telling myself that if I ignore Emmitt, this feeling will go away.

I STAY AWAY FROM EMMITT, and the days bleed together. Kemen crushed tryouts and my little squad of dancers swell to thirty-five girls by the end of the week. And during our warm-up jog on Friday, we hit the curve and Emmitt falls in step with us. Kemen nods his head, greeting Emmitt. I continue with the current course of action, pretending he's invisible.

"Did the professor accept your project?" I ask. The engineering camp has Kemen glued to his desk. He's either researching or coding. It's fascinating to see this side of my son.

"No. He said it doesn't count since I didn't complete all the coding."

"What are you going to do?"

"Submit it anyway."

I stop, huffing and puffing. "What?"

"Come on, Ma." He jogs backwards until I catch up.

"Do the project!"

"I did. He's just hatin'."

"But it could affect your grade."

"It won't matter." He shrugs. "Transferred credits enter as pass or fail and he can't fail me. I have the highest grade in the class."

"See, this is what I'm talking about. I didn't send you to that school to show your ass."

"What's this project?" Emmitt asks.

"I had a team design a video game. The intellectual property is mine, and I hired coders to program it."

"That's dope."

"That's what I'm trying to tell Mom. Do you think Steve Jobs went into the office and programmed the iPhone? Or Bill Gates works in the lab? No, they held the vision and delegated."

"Boy, Imma about two seconds from delegating your ass."

"You'd have to catch me first." Kemen takes off and Emmitt's rolling. His gut-busting laugh and I stop for a second to hear it, then I sprint down the field after my son.

Kemen fakes left, then right, but I'm on him. Then I lunge and get a handful of his shirt. We tumble to the grass, laughing.

"Ma, you almost had me."

"Almost? Boy, please." I roll over, and Emmitt sits on the grass beside me.

"Ma, be nice."

"Kemen, mind your business."

"You are my business." He stops. "It's obvious you two need to talk."

"For the record—"

"You're the parent. I know. But adults need help getting out of their own way too." He jogs over and kisses the top of my head. "Love you, Ma."

"Uh-huh." I watch him head over to meet his friends. "I hate it when he's right."

"And I fucked up." Emmitt picks at something in my hair, and he cups my face in his hands. "What will it take for you to give me a second chance?"

"Tell me the truth."

"I saw you on a date with another man."

"But it wasn't a date."

"It wasn't?"

"No, that was Kemen's father. And why does it matter when you were on a date with Scarlette?"

"It wasn't a date. She was already there, and we started talking about the clinic."

"Yeah, right. That woman wants you."

"And I want you."

The seriousness in his tone takes my breath away. I

haven't slept all week. I've tried talking myself out of this feeling, especially when I know he'll leave town in a few weeks.

"I think we should part as friends."

"I tried but I can't."

"Why?"

Emmitt caresses my face, and I lean into the warmth of his hand. "That's an answer I can't give you. I'm thinking it's your pussy."

I burst out laughing. "No, sir. I can't with you." I jump up. I have a practice to oversee. But Emmitt scoops me up in his arms as if I'm weightless.

"You think I'm joking but I'm deadass serious."

I fall against his chest, laughing.

"You said your pussy would change my life and I'm a believer."

"Bullshit!" He laughs, and I hold on tighter. "You better not drop me."

"Woman, I won't drop you." He sobers and I remove his shades. "Forgive me."

"You're forgiven," I whisper, ignoring the happiness settling in my soul.

"Can I see you tonight?"

I shake my head. "I don't think that's a good idea."

"Please. I'll cook dinner and we could hang out. What's your favorite meal?"

"Anything I don't have to cook."

He chuckles. "Is eight too late?"

I hold his gaze.

"You can trust me, Amber. I won't make that mistake again."

"You better not. And bring ice cream."

I STAND at my board doing a happy dance. Nate gave me fifteen hundred dollars, and with my check from the center, I have twenty-five hundred dollars towards Kemen's tuition. It's a start but nowhere near what I need. I draw a star on my board before taking a quick shower and changing into some sweats.

"Are you staying for dinner?"

"Don't you want to be alone?" Kemen leans against my door.

"Are you okay with me seeing him, as a friend?" I want to say yes, but not throw my kid out.

"I guess, are you okay seeing him, as a friend, when he lives in Dallas?"

"We're not dating. So, yeah."

Kemen gives me a *yeah, right* face that I ignore.

"If you're cool, I'm cool, just don't watch *Creed II* without me."

"All right. We'll watch it tomorrow. You can invite Brandon too."

"And you can invite Coach Emmitt."

"Boy, bye!"

Historically, Saturday nights have been our movie nights. A night we kick back, eat pizza, and close out the world. But this summer, we've hardly had time to sit still. Me working two jobs, him juggling two camps.

He runs out and I grab my laptop. I've been giving some thought to my new side hustle. Thanks to Kemen, I followed some influencers and took notes on how they post on social media. But with a million wanna-be influencers, how can I make it my own and get paid?

I curl into the couch and start researching, and the doorbell rings.

"Ma, Coach Emmitt's here."

"I thought you left."

"We were outside, and he needs help with the groceries."

"Groceries?"

Kemen walks past me into the kitchen, then Brandon enters behind him.

"Hey, Aunt Amber."

"Hey, baby."

I lean against the doorjamb, watching them make another round, and Emmitt enters behind them.

"I hope you're hungry." His smile brightens the room.

"I am. What are you cooking? It's just two of us."

"I didn't know what you liked, and once I started walking down the aisle, food started jumping into my basket."

I chuckle. "Is that so?"

"Yes." He follows the boys into the kitchen, dropping the bags on the counter.

"Leave it to them. They'll handle it."

His gaze swings from Kemen to Brandon. "I'll get out of the way."

"Yeah, they're probably banking on the leftovers. Come have a seat while they earn their keep."

"Yes, ma'am."

We step out of the kitchen when he stops in front of me and kisses me softly on the lips. And my desire for him curls in my stomach. I pull back, looking into his eyes. "What was that for?"

"For not holding last Saturday against me."

"You're welcome."

I smile, watching him head back out and return. And like before, he waves and the vehicle leaves.

"For you."

"Why the car service?"

"To protect your privacy." He passes me a bag and I notice he didn't bring his overnight bag this time.

"You're not staying."

"I didn't want to presume. But I have no problem returning to the hotel in the nude."

I laugh. "You will not. Have a seat while the kids finish." We sit on the couch, and I dig inside the bag he gave me. My fingers brush what feels like lace. I tilt the bag and see lavender lace.

"For the one we ruined."

"We?"

"Yes, we."

I check the tag and it's the right size. That surprises me. I pass him the remote and curl up with my laptop. Emmitt turns on the couch, facing me.

"What are you working on?"

"Her new business," Kemen says, and I roll my eyes.

Emmitt chuckles. "A new business."

"Tell him, Ma. He's a businessman, he could help."

"No, Kemen, he's a guest."

"You always say, first time a guest, second time family." His cocky ass crosses his arms over his chest. "I smelled cologne last weekend."

"Bye! Before I ground you until you're twenty-one." The boys laugh and I'm embarrassed, down to my toes. That boy is going to be the death of me.

"Love you, Ma."

"Love you too and be careful."

They're gone and I'm left with the very amused Emmitt. "Are you going to tell me about this business?"

"It's not a business. Not yet."

"Then what is it?"

I shrug. "An idea."

He leans against the cushion and pulls my feet into his lap. "Tell me about it. I'm a businessman. Maybe I can help."

"Ha ha ha. Kemen's just trying to help." I close my laptop.

"Me too."

Suddenly, I'm shy. I have no clue what I'm looking for, I know clothes and fashion but nothing about starting a business. I tell him the relevant parts of my conversation with Chanel. Emmitt listens and asks questions about my job and what I love about working with the boutique.

"I like spotting new trends before they're hot. I like discovering new brands that cater to all figures and sizes. And I love finding minority owned brands. There's not a lot of them that handle supplying chain stores."

Emmitt holds up a finger and makes a call. "Hey, Jay. You got a second?" He nods, listening on the other end. "I have a friend interested in pursuing business options in the fashion industry."

They go back and forth, and now I'm anxious. Then I hear, "Mind if we stop by?" Emmitt covers the phone. "Is tonight good?"

"Uh… Sure, I guess."

"Bet. Should we bring something? I can do that. We'll be there."

Emmitt stands. "Let's roll. She put the baby down and you'll want to get in all your questions before KJ wakes."

"Wait, you want to ride in my car?"

"Yeah. It's not far. I could call the car service, but it could take them up to a half hour."

I drag my feet, not sure I want fine-ass Emmitt in my hooptie. He wraps an arm around my neck and pulls me in for a hug. And I circle my arms around his waist.

"It's not that bad," he assures me.

"Remember, you said that."

THIRTY MINUTES LATER, we pull into the circle drive of a mansion. Emmitt jumps out and circles the car, opening my door. I can't move.

"Why didn't you tell me to change my clothes? Or comb my hair?" I'm still in joggers, I didn't want Emmitt to assume he was getting laid, and now I'm entering a mansion looking like a bum.

"You have nothing to worry about. They're mad cool. Come on." Emmitt takes my hand.

"I've never been inside a mansion before," I whisper.

"Get ready. It's a beauty. Kamal had it remodeled, and Jayda took almost a year to furnish it. I'll give you a tour." Emmitt rings the doorbell.

"Coach Kamal?"

Emmitt nods and all the facts Kemen spewed give this moment perspective.

"He's my business partner and best friend since junior high. Dean too. We met playing football."

"Did you play professional football together too?"

"We played at the same time. Not on the same teams."

The door opens. "Uncle!"

A little girl jumps, falling forward, and Emmitt scoops her up.

"Hey, Reesie Piecie! Give me some suga." Emmitt kisses all over her face, and the little girl giggles and squirms in his arms. Then she peeks over his shoulder and smiles. "Reese, this is my friend, Miss Amber. Amber, my niece Reese."

"Hi," she sings, and I wave.

"Where are your folks?" Emmitt enters like he owns the place. Reese wraps her little arms around his neck, content in his arms. "King Kamal…."

"Yo, what are you doing here?" Kamal stalls and

smiles over at me. "Hey, Amber. It's nice seeing you. Welcome to my home." He hugs me.

"We're here to see Jay." Emmitt says, and I watch the soothing circle and soft pats on Reese's back.

"She's stretched out by the pool."

"I'm about to throw some steaks on the grills. Y'all staying?"

"No, we don't want to—"

"Yes, we're staying. Do you need to pick up the boys?" Emmitt asks.

"No, Chanel's on duty tonight."

"Bet."

They talk and I follow, struggling to keep my mouth closed. Black art lines the walls. A collection of African vases flank the doors leading to the backyard.

"Jay, I want you to meet someone." Emmitt reaches for my hand, still holding his niece. "This is Amber, Amber this is Jayda. Kamal's wife."

"And my Mommy."

I extend a hand to Jayda.

"Girl, we're huggers around here." She hugs me and offers me a seat. "So, fill me in on your business venture."

Emmitt nods and gives my shoulder a supportive squeeze. I recount the same conversation, but Jayda's questions help me understand why Emmitt wanted us to talk. She's a professional content creator with several international brand deals. The guys hang around the grill talking, and Jayda gives me the tea on how to get started, how to get paid, and how to get free merchandise to feature.

My head swims with the details and it must show on my face.

"It's a lot. Take in what you can and call me when you need me to repeat. It took me years to settle into my process. Have you considered being a stylist?"

"I could. But I need something to work around my son's schedule."

"You have a son?"

"Yeah, let me show you a picture." I search for a picture on my phone, and I hear.

"Amber?"

"Catrina? Oh my goodness, look at you." I hug her, then caress her round belly.

Catrina sits beside Jayda. "Amber and I went to high school together."

"What a small world. You'll have to bring Kemen to Sunday dinner," Jayda insists.

I nod, not making any promises. These are Emmitt's friends and once our little fling is over, I probably won't see them again. The thought sends my eyes to his. Emmitt winks and returns to his beer and conversation.

This is how the rest of the night went. I learn

Catrina is married to Kamal's brother, Rashaad. Dean is married to Kamal's sister, Miya. And the babies, they are adorable. I can't even remember when Kemen was this little.

"And you have two more brothers?" I ask Kamal, still trying to get their names correct.

"Yeah, Quan and Demetrius."

I look over at Emmitt. "Quan from Q's Spot?"

"Yep."

I sit back, watching Emmitt, surrounded by his family. I can't believe I'm having dinner with the Montgomery's from Southern Soul. And they're cool, like Emmitt said. They eat and laugh and talk over each other until the wee hours of the morning. Sometime around midnight, I lean into Emmitt, and before I realize it, I fall asleep to the sound of family and love.

CHAPTER 13

"Amber, wake up." She's curled up into the door, using her hands as a pillow. I hate to wake her, but I need to get her inside the house. She mumbles and gives me the key. Now to figure out which one opens the door.

I try every key thinking about tonight. She fit right in with the others, and it felt natural to have her beside me. The lock clicks and I carry her inside, laying Amber in the bed.

I remove her shoes when she whispers, "Stay."

"I'll be here when you wake."

She falls off to sleep, and I tuck her in bed. Then I head to the living room. I flip through the channels. I hear the shuffling of her feet before she rounds the corner.

"What are you doing up?"

"Coming in here with you." She's wrapped in the comforter from her bed.

I pat the space beside me, and I'm pleased when she lays across my body wiggling until she's comfortable with her face tucked beneath my chin.

"I enjoyed your family." Amber pushes up. "Thank you. It's cool to see Black couples doing it big. Well, and Dean."

"Yeah," Emmitt chuckles. "He's my brother, like Kamal. I don't know where I'd be without those two."

"How'd you meet?" She wiggles again until she exhales. "I could stay here forever."

"And I'd let you."

Amber sits back, staring into my eyes. Questions lurk in her eyes, and I have no answers. I've never felt this way about a woman, and I've never considered anything more than a casual relationship. But with Amber, I find myself wanting more. More of her time. More of her body. More of her.

"I'm listening," she snuggles back up.

"Football brought us together. I was a kid from a group home. Dean was being raised by his nanny while his father traveled the world. Kamal was helping his mother raise his siblings. We're so different, yet football and brotherhood brought us together. And now, man, I'd do anything for those guys."

"They're lucky to have you."

Her words touch a wound I rarely acknowledge. They brought in a rough-around-the-edges kid, and I never wanted to be a burden.

"I think I'm the lucky one. The second Kamal found out about my living situation, the Montgomerys took me in. And his mother, Miss Jackie, single-handedly saved me."

"What do you mean?" Her hand flutters to the side of my neck and I kiss her soft lips.

"I was hellbent on destroying everyone and everything. And she got on my ass, she challenged me by saying, instead of proving the naysayers right, prove them wrong."

"What did she mean?"

"I was fighting, cussing out my teachers. They say hurt people, hurt people. No one wanted to adopt a teenage Black boy. And they wouldn't place me in a foster home because of my behavior. I felt alone in a crowded world. So, I acted out every chance I got. But her words shifted my perspective, and I haven't looked back since, well until last week."

"What happened last week?"

"I got a call from Robin."

"Robin?"

"My mother."

Amber gasps and holds me tighter. She sits up. I search her eyes and all I see is concern. The only people who know this story are Kamal, Dean, and Miss Jackie.

"How'd it go?"

"I flipped the fuck out."

"What?"

"That's the night you saw me in Q's Spot."

"Oh… What did you do?"

"It's not important."

"Emmitt, tonight you called me a friend. Not once, not twice, but several times. I need you to believe that I'd never do anything to hurt you. I'm asking you to trust me."

Trust a woman. I look away, and Amber brings my eyes back to hers. Eyes that remind me of the sun. Then I see her with Kemen, and I know Amber's not like Robin or any woman I've been with.

I exhale. "She called, and I blew up. The sound of her voice makes me feel like that twelve-year-old kid that everyone keeps passing by. Now, my mother, my father, and my blood relatives reach out because I'm a pro football player. They need help with bills or a new car or a loan for a business. None of them gave a damn when I spent holidays alone. I'll cut for Miss Jackie until the day I die, as for Robin…"

"What about Robin?"

"I could care less."

Amber leans forward and kisses me, then she looks me straight in the eyes. "What I'm about to say will probably hurt for a second but in time you'll see I'm right."

I shake my head because I know what she's about to say. My world turns red, and I can't breathe. And I'm on the edge of flipping again.

"Yes, Emmitt. Baby, you have to. You have to forgive her."

"No, I take care of her. I keep a roof over her head. She wants for nothing. She can't say the same towards me and she gave me life. How the fuck do you have a child and just leave? Leave. Go on about your fucking life while I struggled?"

"Emmitt…."

"No, Amber. You don't understand. That's unforgiveable."

"Emmitt, baby, you're building a legacy, and it won't happen with this stain on your heart. Forgive her. Love her. Leave her. Build something new, something beautiful. But leaving it like this isn't an option. Not if you want to reach the peaks of who you are in here." She lays her hand over my heart, and my chest is about to explode. And I know she's right.

"But I don't know how. How do I not be this? Always knowing she gave me away. She had me and didn't choose me." I can't believe I'm spilling my fucking guts. I'm exposing my dark and dirty past, and Amber's unshakeable.

"Start with asking why and listening. I can't speak for her but very few women hold a child in their womb and choose to walk away." She looks away for a second, as if choosing the right words to say.

"Tell me, baby." I hold her tighter. Right now, I'm the closest I've ever been to a human being in my life. To tell her about my hurts and the deepest wound in my soul and I know she cares about me. It's something I never thought I'd have, and suddenly, I do.

"I learned I was pregnant with Kemen when I was sixteen years old. His father didn't want him. My mother didn't want me to have a child. I was told repeatedly how having my child would ruin my life. I listened. Believing the adults in my life knew better. That I'd have children later, after I graduated from college, had a career, had a husband. So, I went to a clinic."

Her body shakes in my arms, and I hold her so tight, I wonder if she can breathe, inhaling the scent of her hair, and I kiss her temple.

"But I couldn't. Every time I closed my eyes, I could see little fingers and little toes. I left that clinic knowing I'd have to raise my child alone. But it didn't stop me from being angry. Emmitt, I was so angry that I got physically ill. And one day, I felt him move. This flutter of life growing inside me. Even at sixteen I knew my life would never be the same."

"Are you close with your mother now?"

She shakes her head. "She came around and helped me so much. Then we lost her a few years ago. And it was like being sixteen all over again. But I'm slowly getting back on my feet."

"What about his father?"

"Nate and I met in high school. He played football, and I was a majorette. He showed me a little attention, and I gave him my virginity." Amber chuckles, but it's the sound of a woman scorn. "I was the thick girl, and he was *the* hot guy. He started whispering sweet nothings in my ear. And I was riding a slippery slope downhill.

"He wanted my cookie, and I wanted a boyfriend to take me to dances and the movies. I had stars in my eyes and his eyes were glued to my ass. I thought we were in a committed relationship. But a positive pregnancy test made my ass grow up with the quickness. That and Nate's girlfriend."

"That you didn't know about?"

"Yep! Talk about awkward. All those late night calls, never having time to hang out, and his excuse was football. Then one day, I stood big as a house in front of the real reason for Nate's absence, his girlfriend. It all made sense. *I was the side chick*."

"Damn, that's fucked up."

"Tell me about it. And I was processing it as a hormonal teenager. I kicked his ass to the curb, determined to raise our son on my own. But it was harder than I expected, and I refused to live on government assistance. So, I dropped out of high school and got a GED."

Amber rolls over until she's laying flat on my chest. "I'm telling you this because no mother is perfect. We're human, always one decision away from a major disaster. But my guess is your mother wants to change your relationship. Why else would she keep calling, knowing you'll blow up? I think she's trying, Emmitt, and if you have even the slightest bit of compassion for all I've endured while raising Kemen, give her a chance to tell her story. And if you still feel the same, at least you tried."

Amber lays her head on my chest, giving me a lot to think about. What if I talked with Robin? It's not as if we don't talk, we've just never discussed how she relinquished her parental rights. We were spotty for years, but I think buying her the house makes her believe everything is all good between us. But it's not. I doubt it will ever be.

The thought of holding this thing against her makes me sick to my stomach. What I don't want is to always have this hanging over me and it leaves me with a major decision. Either talk with her and air this situation out or I can't make Houston my permanent home. I have a few more years in Dallas but I don't want this rage festering in me. Because I'm over my childhood, I survived, I guess it's time to put this Robin situation behind me too.

"You sleep?" Amber whispers and kisses my chest.

"Nah. Thinking about giving Robin a call."

Her head pops up. "I love the sound of that. You know, I could incentivize you."

"Oh really?" I look over at her.

"Yeah, I could plan a nice dinner and—"

"Get the fuck outta here!" I laugh so hard, I cry. Chanel once asked me about the strength of my stomach. It didn't take me long to realize Amber can't cook. And I mean nothing, to the point that Kemen learned to cook from the Food Network because he was tired of microwave meals.

Amber laughs. "I can make some stuff."

"Like what?" I fall back and our laughter fills the air.

"Spaghetti… Pizza… Salad…"

I'm howling because she's serious as fuck. "Salad's not cooking, babe."

"The disrespect," she whines but I can hear the smile in her voice.

Man, it feels good to laugh and just be. I stare up at

the ceiling fan brushing the moisture from my eyes. Then my eyes scan her living room and a sense of calm settles over me.

"So, what about you?" Her questions brings my gaze back to hers.

"What about me?" I roll over on my side facing her.

"Emmitt and Dean are settled down with beautiful families. Do you think you'll join them one day?" The tone in her voice shifts and I wish the room had more light.

"Nah. What's funny is we had a pact, no wife, no kids." My voice trails off as I think about Kamal and Dean, Jayda and Miya. "But I'm happy for them. What about you?"

"What about me?"

"Think you'll get married and have more kids?" The moment the question's out, I don't like the image or the thought of her with another man. That her future and my future aren't the same.

"A part of me wants it. To maybe do it different. I was a kid raising Kemen and I'd like to have the experience as the woman I am today. But I'm not ready for any of that, my hands are full with Kemen and getting him off to college. To get it right."

"Hey, Amber."

"Huh?"

"What's up with you and Kemen?"

"What do you mean?" I hear the smile in her voice, and I slip from beneath her, settling between her thick thighs. She wiggles and I adjust the pillow under her head then trace the features of her face. The thought of pleasing her makes my heart race. Amber is more than I expected. Much more than having fun and life-changing sex. She's the truth.

"I've never seen a mother and son like you two."

"And you never will," she laughs. "I want him to see me as his mother, his friend, and the person who always has his back. And once my mom died, I just made our relationship a safe space for him. He really looks up to you guys on the field and off."

"You're raising an amazing young man."

"I am pretty cool."

"And hot."

"Damn right."

"And—"

Amber covers my lips and I kiss her finger, wondering if this is love. And instead of waiting, I kiss her. I never thought I wanted this feeling, maybe because I didn't trust myself to love a woman. But Amber makes it impossible not to want more than tonight, more than the summer.

She moans, pressing her body into mine and I want to taste her skin. I rock back, removing her shirt, her bra, her joggers, and now her panties. I drop to my knees beside the couch and bring her legs to my shoulders. The spark of passion glowing in her eyes makes me lick my lips, preparing to feast. I lift her pussy to my mouth, and I drag my tongue between her folds, sampling her nectar.

She twists and turns, but I hold on tighter, pushing inside. I work her, one hand teasing her clit, the other playing with her ass. Amber bucks, trying to escape the pleasure. Her head falls back, and I watch the second the orgasm takes hold of her.

"Emmitt..." her fingers dig into the couch, and she gasps begging for release. And like the bastard I am, I withdraw. Her eyes snap open and before she can curse me out, I cover my dick and fill her, dragging us to the carpet. She's riding me and my hands roam every curve of her body.

"I love your body... I love your thighs... I love your ass..." I flip her on her back, and I whisper across her lips. "I love you, Amber."

I don't wait. Not caring if she doesn't return my love. Not when my heart feels alive and at peace for the first time in my life. We move as if we've made love a million times, and when her pussy grips me tight, I plan to make her crazy with need, crazy with lust, crazy until she loves me too.

Our love making shifts to mating. I'm a man on a mission and she's a woman with a plan. And I plan to show her our paths don't have to run parallel, not when we feel like this.

Her cries flood my ears, and I growl my release. I pull her to me, and I whisper forever across her lips. "You're mine, Amber."

"And then what?" She huffs, her golden eyes looking to me for the answers.

"Just let me love you, baby."

"Okay."

CHAPTER 14

EMMITT'S REQUEST SOUNDS SIMPLE. And I'm not about to complicate it. But my heart questioned how long when he lives in Dallas, and I live in Houston. The drive is at least four hours, and once the school year starts, our schedule is stuffed with Kemen's sports. This fling of ours isn't really a fling anymore. I don't have a name for it and that makes it easier to pretend like time isn't running out.

I arrive at the last boutique for the week and flick on the lights. I'm the first one to arrive. I walk the floors, checking the current displays, using my phone to minimize my time. Snapping pictures means I can work through the redesigns in my head, pull the new outfits, and restyle the mannequins. Then I work on my reports over the weekends, mainly making suggestions for new inventory based on sales, trends, and my personal recommendations.

I review the photos and decide to redress all the mannequins. It will take twice the time I allocated, so I set the timer. I stack the outfits in front of said doll, and right when I prepare to dress them, I think about some advice from Jayda and I turn on my camera.

I step to the mannequins and talk to my cellphone camera. I explain my process and hold up each garment and close the video with my top three tips. *That wasn't bad.* Then I notice the time. I can't be late. Emmitt and his no tardy rule have rubbed off. Me, the queen of "nothing starts on time", is benefiting from arriving early because it's the little pocket of time I have alone with my guys. Our warm-up run gives us time to catch up on the day and… My eyes sting with unshed tears.

"Don't. You got shit to do. Move your ass, Amber." I tell myself, rushing through the rest of the process, putting all of the dolls where they belong.

How'd I let myself fall in love? I'm not in love. I'm not.

I'm not. He's just sort of fantastic. I drop to the floor, giving myself a moment. The image of Emmitt's smile, the sound of his laughter, the feel of his touch. But he's not mine to have. Good luck telling my heart.

"Ugh. What choice do you have, Amber?" I brush away a tear. The thought of Emmitt leaving grips my heart. "I can cry like a baby or have fun while he's here."

I don't like the choices. But it is what it is. My eyes settle on a slither of lavender fabric across the room and an idea sparks. I stumble to my feet with a smile on my face.

"Oh Emmitt, I'm about to give you something to remember."

KEMEN and I arrive at the center. He runs inside to change clothes and I gather my equipment. We've graduated to a larger speaker and props. The girls want to perform at the banquet, and surprisingly, Scarlette approved the request. Once I have my rolling cart loaded, I push it towards the field.

"Amber."

I glance over my shoulder. "Scarlette."

"Have a second?"

The voice in my head is getting froggy. But I'm keeping it classy because we need that scholarship. Kemen's been on time to practice, they voted him the captain of the team, and his coaches love him. Even with working the extra hours at the boutique in the mornings and coaching the girls in the evenings, I'm still ten grand from Kemen's tuition for Jordan Prep.

So, I plan to play nice until she calls his name at the banquet. The thought of having seven grand free and clear in my bank account makes me paste a smile on my face.

"Sure. What's up?"

"Emmitt."

I hear tires screeching to a stop. Even with our lack of a title, everything about Emmitt Booker is stamped *mine*. "What about him?"

"I think there's a misunderstanding." A soft smile touches her lips but stank lingers in her eyes. "Emmitt and I started seeing each other last summer. And we were fine until you started coaching the girls. So, what's it going to take for you to back off of my man?"

Her man? I chuckle. My petty is the best you'll find in H-Town. But I'm not about to let this woman get under my skin. I bat my lashes and smile back. "Emmitt and I are friends and coworkers."

"That's how you want to do this?" Scarlette stares down at me.

"There's nothing to do."

Kemen exits the building and heads in our direction.

"Your little fling isn't worth my time. He'll be back." Her nice-nasty smile has the hood Amber ready to act a fool. But this woman is the difference between my child attending public school or private school.

"I guess you'll have to wait your turn." I smile when her fake-ass smile drops. "Are you done?"

"Yes, you can get back to work. Have a great practice."

I'm fuming. Who does she think she is? I knew she had a thing for Emmitt, but now I'm wondering if they've been seeing each other the entire time.

"You good, Ma?"

"Yeah."

I move with a low-grade fire burning in my gut. That woman has some fucking nerve. I set up for the girls and turn to jog with Kemen. We settle into a comfortable pace and my mind's replaying the conversation. This is why I should have left him alone. I don't need this petty high school shit in my life.

"Hey, babe."

I look up, and my grimace erases the smile off his face. We jog with Kemen holding down most of the conversation. Stupid me. Again. I think we're on the same page and he's kicking it with me and her. I mean, it's highly probable. He's spent Friday nights and some Sundays at the house. But he has five other nights to fuck whomever he wants, and it's not my business because he's not my man. I basically signed up to be a fucking side chick. I stop. What the fuck am I doing?

Kemen notices and turns back around.

"Keep going." I fold over, catching my breath.

"You sure?"

"Yeah. Finish your laps and have a good practice."

Kemen runs off but Emmitt stays.

"What's going with you?"

"Nothing. I just need a second."

Emmitt crosses his arms over his chest. A chest I know well. I've fallen asleep to the sound of his heartbeat and awaken to the same. *But it's only temporary.* His steamy gaze travels over my body and I'll be damned if I don't want to fuck him. This was supposed to be a fun thing. Not a forever thing, and I knew that going in.

"Baby, what's going on?" He walks closer, as if hearing the war going on inside my head.

"Don't call me baby." I whisper, holding up a hand up to stop him. I can't let him touch me.

"Why?"

"I have practice." I walk off, and he's on my heels. Then he runs around me, blocking my escape.

"You expect honesty, yet you're lying to me."

I freeze. "It's not the same thing."

"Bullshit. Let's leave the games on the field. What's this about?" His gaze burns through me.

The reality of our situation is clear. He's three weeks away from returning to Dallas. I'm not about to fuck up my life over some dick.

"I don't have the capacity to deal with this or you or her." I walk off again.

"What the fuck does that mean?" Emmitt questions, but doesn't stop me, and suddenly, I'm not having fun anymore.

I sit on the floor with Chanel working on my hair. This is our girl chat time and I need it. Girl chat and lots of wine except she's yelling at the movie.

"I'm supposed to believe the prostitute lands a millionaire and I keep fucking broke dudes?" Chanel says.

"I can't believe you've never seen *Pretty Woman*."

"And you wonder why?" She's tugging on my locs and I'm counting the costs.

Emmitt is a catch. He's handsome, funny, and driven. He can be harsh when he's stressed and a hothead when he's angry, but it's because he's passionate. Passionate people have high highs and low lows, and he's no exception. And Emmitt knows my body like no other man, and I can't pinpoint the moment, but somewhere along the way, I gave him my heart.

"Is it so bad to think that you could meet someone unexpectedly and make it work?"

"No, but that's not what this movie's selling. It's

selling a dream that's *never* going to happen." She points at the tv. "He met her on the track. He paid her for her cookie. That sounds like a transaction to me."

I shake my head. "You're missing the point."

"Stop moving your head."

"I feel Vivian's situation. It's like this fling with Emmitt." I tilt at an awkward angle. "I'm not a prostitute but my world is nothing like his. I'm a single mother who can barely pay her bills. I have a GED and bad credit."

"Girl, that doesn't compare to prostitution. You're a real woman with real woman shit to deal with."

"But at some point, I have to take my head out of the clouds and see it as temporary. We're having fun, and in two weeks, he'll return to his life, and I'll continue to live mine."

God, that hurts.

"You act like you can't call or visit. There's email and video chat."

"But we'll have nothing in common. Our only connection is the clinic. And then what?"

Chanel huffs and loosens her grip on my hair. "Stop selling yourself short. You're beautiful, smart, got a bangin' body. You're an amazing mother. He'd be lucky to have you."

"Thank you."

She works on my hair, and I watch the movie when a text comes through from Emmitt. I stare at it.

"What would you do?"

"Me? Girl, I'm the last one you need to take advice from. I have Trent and Lawrence—"

"Lawrence?"

"Please, don't ask because it's a hot-ass mess." Her voice shakes, and I look up at her. "I'm okay. Just torn."

I turn back, trying not to roll my eyes.

"What, cow?" she yells.

"All I have is one word."

"What?"

"Whataburger."

We laugh and laugh, and I can't stop. "See, I can't tell your ass nothing."

"Yes, you can, because I'll love you, anyway. That man is a nonfactor."

"But Trent is so different. He wants me to meet his family. What do I look like going to see the Brady Bunch?"

"You look like a woman open to new experiences and love."

"I don't know." She rolls her eyes. "What are you going to do?"

"Enjoy the ride while it lasts."

CHAPTER 15

I ARRIVE at Q's Spot to meet with my boys, but I'm not in the mood. Amber stormed off, and I gave her room. But she hasn't answered my phone calls or my text messages.

"Fuck it." I head inside and see Demetrius, another one of Kamal's brothers. Miss Jackie has four sons and one daughter. But he's the brother I know the least about since he bounces in and out of town. "What's good with you?"

He stands and we hug. "I'm in town for a few days. Kamal said everyone was meeting here."

"Yeah, Jayda gave him the night off." We laugh and I take the seat beside him. "How's everything going?"

"Good. I'm heading to Los Angeles."

"Word? What's in LA?"

"I've contracted to work security for a few months."

"I know you're a writer, but how does all of this work?" We stop and order a couple of beers, and I wait for his response.

"Which part?"

"All of it."

Demetrius nods and takes a drink of his beer. "I approach writing like a method actor. So, I usually work through what I believe the story will be about and then I pitch it to my agent. He shops it, and once I get a contract, I submerge myself in the subject matter. Then I live that life for three months to half a year, it depends."

"That's crazy. It's like you get to live nine lives."

"Yeah, it's something like that."

"And that's why you're going to LA?"

"Yes, I'm contract to work private security for an actress shooting a movie out there."

"Security?" I guess I shouldn't be surprised. Demetrius is quiet but strong in presence.

He nods. "Yeah, I've been training with a firm for the last year."

"Damn. That's cool. But it sounds dangerous."

"No more than you running around on the field with a football and a helmet."

I laugh. "I guess you're right. Anyone I know?"

"Kanesha Greene."

"What?" I sing. "I met her once out in New York. How'd you get an A-list celebrity?"

"Cause I know people. And her current guard is going on maternity leave. So, the timing worked."

"Yo! The room's ready." Q calls out.

We head back, and I drop to the couch.

"Marriage must make you late." Q jokes. We grasp hands and tap shoulders. Q always has a smile on his face.

"That and kids."

We settle around the table, and I'm loving the vibe Q has with this club. His other location is more like a traditional club. This place is a cross between a club and a lounge.

"Rumor has it that you're opening another spot."

"Yeah. I have Rashaad looking for another building. I'm thinking a strip mall."

"To buy?"

"Yeah. 'Shaad and I think it's time. Buy the strip and lease out the other spaces."

"Damn, that's lit. Let me know if you looking for a partner."

Q leans back with a chuckle. "We can talk now and bring your wallet."

"*Shhiiid*, you ain't said nothing but a thang. You in, Demetrius?" And I'm not kidding. I want my portfolio tight before I walk away from football, and I have a few years to do it.

"You know it. You might want to hold off because Kamal and Dean will definitely want a chance to contribute." He looks between us. "I think this would be great. And if Rashaad's looking, why stop at a strip mall?"

The energy circling the room is better than being on the football field. This is why I hang with these men. We laugh, shoot the shit, eat, party, *and* get money. Which brings me to the conversation I had with Amber today. She was tripping, and I let her ass slide. Things have been tense the closer we get to the end of the clinic, and I wish she'd just level with me. Something's going on in that beautiful mind of hers, and I'm not a mind reader. So, I fall back until she's ready to let me in.

I grunt and order a shot.

"What's that about?" Demetrius turns in his chair, and I realize we're alone. "Q went to place our food order and check on the floor."

I consider how much I want to share about my situation with Amber. He's family in my book and I need to see this relationship, or whatever it is, clearly before I make another move. I'd usually discuss it with Kamal and Dean, but they've gone from a roster of women to one. I'm not on team marriage, but I can't fully explain the feelings I have for Amber. This is out of my wheelhouse.

"Don't overthink it. Start at the top and don't leave anything out. I catch on quick." Demetrius takes a drag of his beer.

"I met a woman, a very beautiful woman. We hit it off and I've been seeing her for about a month."

"Exclusively?"

I run a hand over my goatee. "I mean, yeah. Pretty much. Not intentionally."

"But you're not skirt chasing?" His level gaze reminds me of Kamal.

"Since you put it like that, no. I've been busy with the clinic and kicking it with her."

"Hum. Continue."

I stare at him and go on telling him about Amber and her contribution to the clinic. Her sense of humor, her independence, and her drive. "It's crazy to see all that she juggles, and she's still laid back."

"Did she know who you were before you guys hooked up?"

"She knew I play pro ball but Amber still wasn't checking for me." I laugh as the memory of us on the football field comes back to me. "If it wasn't for Kemen, she would have ran in the opposite direction."

"Kemen?"

"Her son."

"She has a kid and you've been dating her consistently?"

"Not *really* dating. But yeah."

"Hum."

"That's the second hum. What does that mean?" I sit forward, a little anxious. Demetrius is quiet but has a direct manner that's like a sharp knife. You don't realize you're cut until you see the blood.

"What does what mean?" Q drops into the chair. Demetrius gives a quick recap, and they face me. One with a stern face, the other ready to bust a joke.

"I'm surprised that you'd seriously date a single mother."

"Why? I don't discriminate. I like my women in all shapes and sizes. All ethnicities."

"You like to fuck them. Fucking is not dating." Demetrius cuts me so quick I don't have a response.

"Well, damn. I should have got some popcorn."

"Q, your ass it crazy." I laugh.

"Don't tell me you're next." Q holds his heart.

"Nah. I'm standing strong."

"That shit sound weak than a mutha…"

I laugh and I'm with him. The more time I spend with Amber, the more my resolve to remain unattached feels like the wrong decision.

"Why are you surprised, Demetrius?" I face him.

"You sure you want to know my answer."

"I asked."

He shrugs. "You have mother issues."

I stall and flickers of red cloud my vision.

"Don't get pissed. Most people have relationship issues caused by parental factors and you're not the only one."

"So, you're saying you don't date because of Ma?" Q asks, building a bridge between what Demetrius said and what he inferred.

"Hell, yeah. You do too."

"I didn't ask to be psychoanalyzed. What's your issue?" The brothers stare at each other, neither smiling, neither talking until Demetrius exhales.

"Trust."

"And Ma's the reason?"

"Give or take."

"How's that?"

"The underlying reason for their divorce doesn't always match my memories."

I sit back, listening. I've seen Miss Jackie and Mr. Kenneth together over the years. And watching the siblings work through their remarriage has been challenging.

Q nods his head. "Do you plan to talk with her about it?"

"One day. For now, she's happy and Kenneth's happy."

"But are you happy?"

"Now who's psychoanalyzing whom?" A ghost of a smile lingers on Demetrius' face, but his eyes look unconvinced.

"You're not the only Montgomery with a degree in this bitch." We laugh and silence returns. We're all trapped in our own thoughts.

"I think I'm there with you." I speak up. "How am I supposed to trust a woman when I can't trust my mother? And every woman I've been with has wanted me for one of two reasons: my dick or my money and nowadays it's both. And I get it. We all want something. But I'm not about to wife a chick just so she can have access to my bank account."

"And you believe Amber's after your money?" Demetrius asks.

"No, not at all."

"Then why would you lump her in the same group with those other women?" He rocks forward, leaning on the table. "You said she didn't know who you were. You said she's genuine, independent, and takes care of her son. How does any of that compare to your other entanglements?"

The truth of his words makes me feel like an asshole. "But in those other situations, I came and went as I pleased. There wasn't baby's father sitting around sniffing behind them."

"You jealous? Your stroke game getting weak in your old age?"

"Q, your ass is always instigating. No, my dick game ain't lacking."

"Then what's the problem? A good woman will always have men sniffing around her. Believe me, if she wanted to fuck that dude, she would, and he'd let her. Dudes are basic like that." Q, the straight shooter.

Demetrius nods like he's about to bring us home. "So, the question is, can you trust her? Because you're not concerned about the kid's father. Women have no issue finding sex. We think it's all about the dick but it ain't. They want fidelity, protection, and financial support. They want a man to want more than their bodies and their jewel."

"Who are you?" I joke, but he's given me a lot to think about.

"Demetrius Montgomery." He returns to his beer.

"Damn, big bro, drop the mic then…." Q howls, laughing.

"And Emmitt, if you want to be with her, tell her. And if it's meant to be, it will be. That's on God."

We put my situation with Amber aside when Kamal and Dean finally arrive. The plan for moving forward with the strip mall is confirmed and Rashaad agrees to find us a property.

I keep one ear on the conversation, but my mind is

replaying my conversation with Demetrius. Who would have thought that he would get me straight? I chuckle. And send Amber a text message.

I'm still at Q's. Want to join me for a drink? I put my phone away and look up to find myself alone with Kamal and Dean.

"What's up with you tonight?" Kamal asks.

"Man, it's been a long month. What about you? How are you feeling about approaching end of the clinic?"

"I'm feeling good about our first attempt. But I think we'll need to scout another partner for the next one," Kamal says.

Dean nods, sitting beside me. "The field could be larger. I love the staff, but it's always difficult to onboard a new program when you're using an existing staff. They have to unlearn old ways and I think they've done a stellar job with adapting, but next time I'd vote for a dedicated staff, even if they're only seasonal."

"How about the budget?" I look over at Kamal.

"You've done well. Even with adding the majorette squad, which is a nice touch. How's that going? You and Amber."

Dean laughs in his hand, and I drop my head back.

"Man, we're still hanging out. I'm feeling her but…. We'll see." I shrug. After the talk I had with Demetrius and Quan, I think it's time to talk with

Amber. "But I have a question for you. Did you have any doubts about dating Jay once you realized she had a child?"

"But you've dated women with children before."

"I'd use the word date loosely. But I never interacted with their kids other than a hi and bye."

"And now?" Dean asks.

"I guess I'm trying to decide if we're meant for the summer or more."

Kamal nods. "Well, with Jay, I knew about Reese early on." He smiles as if seeing a fond memory and continues. "When dating a single mother, you have to be selfless. They're not like other women who'll jump when you call. But on the flip side, I saw the full extent of Jayda's capacity to love. Jay does everything for Reese and KJ. And I rest better knowing my children will always know love. It's who Jay is."

My boy is head over hills in love with his wife and it's written all over his face. I've never seen either of them so happy and at peace. Is this what I can expect if I'm willing to give this relationship a shot?

"And think about it this way, you get Amber *and* Kemen." Kamal continues, "I can't imagine my life without Reese. That little girl grabbed my heart and she has it wrapped around her little fingers. And I would have missed out on seeing this wonderful little human with a heart that's…."

"What are y'all doing to my brother?" Q reenters the room. "The king has officially left the building."

Talk about the upcoming season and Rashaad's search for property resumes and I'm officially off the hook. But Amber didn't return my text or my call. I hang around at the bar after the others leave, chatting with Q when he asks, "Isn't that your girl?"

I exhale, Amber came. I turn around.

"May I join you?"

I stare at Scarlette, wrapped in a sexy gold dress. I'm disappointed and it's no one's fault but my own. She resembles the women who wait for my calls, who jump at the chance to have dinner with me, who do everything I want, when I want it. This is what I used to want, but I don't anymore.

"I'm about to leave, but I'll have one last drink with you. Have a seat."

Scarlette grins and the fragrance of her perfume smells like temptation. "I heard you mention drinks tonight, but I don't see the others."

"You missed them."

"Oh, too bad." Her hand covers my knee and drags up my thigh. I grab her wrist. "How about a nightcap?"

"Scarlette, what is it you're after?"

"You."

This woman must be hard of hearing. "I'm trying to keep this professional. To keep our working situation straight. I've told you repeatedly that I'm not looking for a relationship."

"I've seen you with Amber." Her eyes glow with envy. "But what I know, that you don't, is it will never work. Now me, I'll upgrade you. This camp is only the beginning."

"Never disrespect Amber again." I stand up, dropping a bill on the bar. Then I turn to leave. I knew she'd try again, but damn.

"Or what?"

I spin around. "Fuck with me and find out. Good night, Scarlette."

HOURS LATER, I sit awake thinking about my day. Letting Amber walk away. Talking with Demetrius and Quan. Receiving advice from Kamal and Dean. But it's Kemen that rises to the surface. His words cut through the noise of my past clashing with my present.

… adults need help getting out of their own way too.

That and the gift of having both Amber and Kemen in my life. Not just for the summer, but for the foreseeable future. Before, the thought would fuck me up, but tonight, it feels as welcoming as the softness of my woman's thighs. It feels like where I belong.

I know it's late, but I dial Amber's number.

"Hello…" Her sleepy voice lightens the weight of my decision.

"Babe…"

"Emmitt, is everything okay?"

"Yeah, I love you."

"Don't—"

"Is Kemen home?"

"No."

I sit forward. "You have a choice: I can make love to you here or there. Pick.

Amber releases a shaky breath. "There."

"I'll have a car in your driveway in twenty minutes."

CHAPTER 16

I HOLD my overnight bag tight. The driver stops in front of the hotel and I climb out, not sure how this will land. I'm all for sexcapades. I'll throw my tricks on a dude to make his head spin. But I've never done this before.

I stroll inside the lobby, captivated by the chandeliers and the elegant lobby. The elevator climbs until I'm standing outside his door. I take a cleansing breath and knock on the door. While I wait, I admire the table with an oversize ceramic vase. I run a finger on the detail carvings etched on the table when the door opens behind me.

Emmitt's standing in a towel. Freshly showered. My eyes follow the lines of his lean body, and my stupid ass almost missed this.

"Are you going to stand out here all night?"

"No." I step forward and he reaches for my bag.

"I need to hold on to this."

He gives me a suspicious look, and I enter the room. The sight steals my breath. Candles glow around the room. His arms circle around my waist and he pulls me close. Emmitt feathers kisses up my neck, and my eyes slide closed.

"Why are you wearing a jacket?" He notices, pulling back.

I turn in his arms. "Unwrap your gift."

Heat fills his eyes. "My gift?"

I nod and step back to give him room. He unties the strap around my waist and holds the sides of my jacket open. A hush falls over him.

His hands run over my shoulders, and I stand in front of him in a sheer red lace bustier with garters.

"Turn around."

I turn slowly. I'm wet from the glint of pleasure in his eyes and the wood beneath his towel.

"Fuck…"

I glance over my shoulder as he appreciates the thong panties. Emmitt drags a hand over my bare cheeks.

"There's more."

His eyes lock with mine. "More what?"

His dick jumps under the towel, and I reach for the small fold near his navel. There's something about the way he looks at me. My skin is on fire and my pussy purrs, waiting for daddy to handle his business. The towel floats to the floor and I join it.

"I've missed this dick."

I take him in my mouth. This wasn't part of the plan. But the scent of his fresh skin, the moisture clinging to his skin, and the sight of his thick, long, perfect dick requires a detour. I go down on my man. He holds my head, I grip his cheeks, and he drills in my mouth.

And for a second, I realize this could be the last time. The last time I taste him, the last time I have him. *Give him something to remember*, a naughty voice whispers and I suck harder. His shaft gliding over my lips, tapping the back of my throat, and I roll his full balls in my hand.

"Fuck…."

I can't say shit, my mouth is full. My hand slips inside my folds and I deep throat him and stroke myself. And he jerks, trying to slip from my grip. I hold tighter. He drives, and my eyes water from the force.

Once…

Twice…

And I glance up, swallowing.

"Oh, your ass is mine…"

. . .

AMBER DRAINS me dry and sits back on her heels with a smile on her face. I scoop her up in my arms.

"I have another outfit."

"I don't give a damn." I drop her on the bed and cover myself and drive into her wet pussy. I circle deeper and deeper, sucking on her shoulder, her neck, then I push her face to the mattress.

Her screams muffle into the covers as she holds on for this ride. I'm aiming for her soul through her guts. The sound of my hips slamming against her ass echoes around us.

Amber's mine. This pussy is mine. I don't care what I have to do. She'll be mine. Forever.

My eyes open. I can't be serious. And the feel of her pussy gripping my dick brings me back. That's what I want. Resolved, I push my lady to the edge, and it's just the beginning.

I FALL FLAT OUT and roll over to see Emmitt covering himself again. "You can't possibly want to do it again."

"I do, and we will. Open your legs for me, baby."

I spread my legs. He drags a warm towel over me before he's back inside me. We're eye to eye. His hands anchored against the mattress, and he's staring into my soul. "Be with me, Amber."

"I *am* with you, Emmitt."

"… as my woman."

I move to stop his stroking when another release swirls in my core. He holds my face, not allowing me to turn from his penetrating gaze. This is what I want, but it's four years too soon. And the world around me crumbles in sweet surrender, and I know this is over.

"Emmitt…" I scream, unable to control the shutter through my body.

He lays, pulling me into his strong arms. His heart thumps against my back. "Say yes, Amber."

I shake my head. "How Emmitt?"

"I'll take care of it."

"No…" I pull away, sitting up to face him. "I'm listening."

"You can come to Dallas."

This isn't the fantasy.

"I can't do that. I have a child and he has school." I slide to the edge of the bed. "Emmitt, thank you for asking, and in another lifetime, I would have gladly packed my bags. But I can't."

"Then we can travel. You can come there, and I can come here."

"When? Kemen plays football and runs track."

"You're not going to at least try?"

"I told you. My son comes first."

"I'm not trying to come between you and Kemen. I'm asking whether you have room in your life for me."

I think about his question and answer honestly. "No, I don't."

Emmitt laughs, and it's not the laughter that makes my heart flutter. This laugh crushes any hope we have to being something more than summer sex buddies.

"Then what the fuck are we doing?"

"We're supposed to be having fun. This was supposed to be some good sex and laughs. I didn't ask for this."

"Well, neither did I. I think you should go."

My heart twists in a knot. I slip from the bed, still slick from our lovemaking. Why did I even bother? Because I love him. But love isn't enough. I had love, and that love left me raising a son on my own, struggling, and I'm not about to throw a grenade into my life again.

"Emmitt, I'm sorry."

"Don't be sorry. You warned that your pussy would change my life. Congratulations."

I jerk away from him. "This is not how I wanted tonight to end."

"But it did. Should I call you a cab?"

"No." I look around for my bag and when I turn back.

Emmitt is gone.

CHAPTER 17

THE NEXT TWO weeks are a blur. The clinic ends with all the boys walking across the stage at the banquet, collecting their participation trophies. The majorettes dance and Scarlette surprises us all when she offers Amber the role of dance instructor for the next school year.

I even had my first real conversation with Robin. We're still rocky, but she's planning to visit me in Dallas, and we've agreed to start fresh. The hours can't move fast enough until I look over and see Amber with Kemen's father.

"Congratulations, son." Miss Jackie hugs me tight. "I think you told me about this when you were sixteen. I knew you would do it."

I smile down at her. "It's surreal, and the kids had a blast."

"And what about you?"

I glance over at Amber. "It was life changing."

"Talk to her."

"And say what?"

"I'm sorry for calling you a whore and an opportunist."

"Damn, Miss Jackie."

"What? You asked." She chuckles, but the truth in her eyes makes my heart ache. "A misunderstanding wrecked my life for twenty years. So, my advice sounds harsh, but it could save you from a colossal mistake."

"What happened?"

Her eyes water. "Promise you'll let me tell the others."

I nod, not sure what I'm agreeing to.

"I slept with Kenneth's best friend."

Her words wash over me, and I remember Demetrius' confession about his inability to trust women. "You don't have to explain."

"I do." Tears roll down her cheeks, and she wipes them away, trying to finish the story. "It was a mistake, and he was willing to forgive me, but I couldn't find the guts to forgive myself."

I wrap an arm around her, pulling her to my chest. Robin and I could mend our relationship. And I'll always be grateful to Amber for encouraging me to talk with Robin. But this woman will always be my mother.

"Miss Jackie, thank you. For sharing this story and for helping me become the man I am. I may not work things out with Amber, but I've healed from all those bad memories and I'm ready to move on."

"I'm proud of you."

We hug and Miss Jackie returns to her table and I walk over to Amber on the dance floor.

"May I?"

Kemen looks up. "Sure, coach."

"No, I'd rather not," Amber says.

"I'm boarding a plane in about an hour, and I'd like to talk with you before I leave."

Kemen turns over his mother to me and I wrap her in my arms. And for the last time, I hold her, smelling her hair and staring into her amber eyes.

I open my mouth to apologize, and she starts. "I love you, Emmitt. And I knew it when I left your place, and I know it more than ever now. But love isn't enough. And when you tack on distance, your career, and my son, it is unrealistic and unfair to ask either of us to move beyond this moment."

"You could have tried."

"I did. Going to you was me trying. Juggling Kemen and dance and work was me trying. Could you imagine me trying to do that with over two hundred miles between us?"

We dance and I think about her words.

"You travel for your job and I'm running Kemen from place to place. We'll never see each other. And first, we'll argue, and then, you'll find someone who can do all the things I can't."

"That's not fair."

"But it's the truth. We have sex nonstop and you expect me to think you'll suddenly stop because I'm not there? I'm not falling for that one again."

"No, I expect you to trust me. That I'm a man of my word."

"And that's the nail in our coffin. Because I know you're a man of your word."

I look down at her. "What?"

"Emmitt, I want more than great sex. I want to get married and have kids. Maybe not now but I want the option. And you don't."

"You're selfish, Amber. You're taking my words, abusing them. Padding this story to allow you to hide and make me out to be the bad guy. But the plot twist you're forgetting is I love you. And I would have done anything to make you happy. But I guess we'll never know." I kiss the top of her head. "Goodbye, Amber."

I walk away from the only woman I've loved. The guys stay and agreed to represent DEK Ventures. My work here is done, and training camp starts tomorrow.

CHAPTER 18

I FUCKED UP. And I can't separate my insecurities about how I could ever be the person he needs and the responsibility I have for my son. I return to the table, numb.

"Was that Emmitt Booker?" Nate asks.

"Yes."

"You should have got his autograph for me. I love that man."

"Yeah... *me too.*"

He looks at me with a weird expression, and then the lights dim. A collective gasp rolls across the room, and I see Coach Trent kneeling before Chanel with a small box. Her eyes find me, and I nod my head. In my head, I scream, *Leap! Don't be afraid of love.*

Chanel accepts, and the crowd claps. I run over and hug my friend.

"Hey, what happened with Emmitt? What did you tell him?"

"Goodbye."

"Oh, Amber…" She wraps me in a hug so tight, my eyes water. "You'll be all right."

"I know. It just hurts like hell. But this is not about me. Let me see your rock."

We laugh and giggle. Chanel will be a beautiful bride. We hug once more, and I return to my seat.

THE CEREMONY BEGINS and Kemen wiggles anxiously in his seat.

"Don't worry, son. You got this." Nate encourages him, resting an arm behind my chair. He came tonight because he heard I was dating someone. I shake my head. He'd probably beg to marry me if he knew it was his beloved Emmitt Booker. But that's over.

Scarlette stands behind the podium to announce the scholarships. Brandon is the first called. We're up on our feet, clapping and screaming for him. Another kid is called and then another. And neither are Kemen.

"Can I use your phone?" he whispers.

"Yeah." I pass it to him, waiting.

I stare at Scarlette letting her know without words that I'm coming for that ass. And this trick winks at me.

"I'm going to kill her."

"Amber, don't make a scene," Nate says.

"Shut up, Nate." I turn to Kemen. "How are you, baby?"

"I'm fine."

I scan the program and she's nearing her closing remarks. I slide to the end of my chair. "Kemen, if something happens to me, I want you to live with your Aunt Chanel."

Scarlette wishes us safe travels and good night, and I jump to my feet.

"Ma, stay right here. It's fine."

"No, I have something to say to her."

"WWJD?" My damn son asks.

"He would whip her ass."

I dart through the crowd with one person in mind. Chanel warned me. Scarlette did that shit on purpose, and I should be the bigger person, but I can't. Not after getting so close, and now we'll have to give up Kemen's seat at Jordan Prep. I don't stop until I'm standing at the bottom of the stairs waiting for her.

Scarlette freezes.

"Did my relationship with Emmitt factor into your scholarship decision?"

"No," she laughs. Then she steps around me and glances back. "You know he'll fuck women like you and marry a woman like me."

"Fuck you and your job offer. Find another dance instructor."

"You really should watch your mouth. That's why your son doesn't have his scholarship now."

"Oh, bitch, I know you didn't—"

I reach for her, and I'm blocked.

"Emmitt." I almost don't recognize Scarlette's breathy tone.

"You've officially received the final donation from DEK Ventures."

A hush falls over the room, and Scarlette's eyes are bucked out of her head.

Emmitt turns to Kemen. "Thanks for calling me. Do me a favor?"

"Sure, coach."

"Email me your school information. I got you, but you have to promise to not give your mother fits about your projects." Emmitt extends his hand.

"Emmitt, you don't have to—"

"Amber, this isn't about you. Kemen earned it."

I nod and step aside, and Nate elbows me, trying to get an introduction.

"Uh, Emmitt Booker, this is Nate Russell, Kemen's father."

"I'll accept if you let me intern for DEK Ventures over school breaks and next summer."

"Always negotiating. You get it honestly." Emmitt

laughs, and my heart still flutters. "Deal." They bump fists and hug. "All right, Young King, I got a plane to get."

"Good luck at training camp."

"You don't need luck when you're prepared."

Kemen laughs, and Emmitt turns and walks away. I stand like an idiot.

"He just saved your ass." Chanel's standing over my shoulder.

"I know."

"Then why are you standing here? Use some of that damn unicorn magic and go get your man."

"But I already told him no."

"Look, I'm about to marry a White guy. And I'm going to rock his White world."

"You are wrong on *soooooo* many levels."

"And it's why you love me. Now, go get your man, Amber Evans."

I run. Thankful for every lap I ran this summer. And I'm not winded. Okay, I'm a little winded, but I'm not stopping. I can see Emmitt near the glass door, and I call out to him.

"Emmitt, stop."

He moves for the door. I kick off my heels and run faster.

"I'm running in an evening gown, and you're determined to make me chase you."

"Only you would complain about running after me when you broke things off with me because you're scared."

I stop. Now I'm huffing, and judging by the look on his face, he's pissed, and I don't blame him. "Emmitt, I apologize. But look at this from my perspective. You're a rich, handsome, and caring man. You travel the country, and you have access to anything and everything you could ever want.

"I am a single mother who juggles her bills, I've never been outside of Texas, most days I'm praying my car makes it to my destination, and I might need to find another part-time job. Because the struggle out here is *real*." I laugh to keep from crying.

I take a step towards him.

"And I didn't want to be like all the other people who are waiting around for your money. Or that you'd wake up one day and resented asking me into your life. I couldn't let that happen to us."

"So, you're basically saying the D changed your life?" A smile brighter than the brightest days spreads across his face. And he laughs, and God, my soul is complete.

"No, that's not what I'm saying. I'm saying…. I love you too, and I'm scared that saying yes will change my life, but I don't want to live life without you."

"Come here."

Emmitt kisses me, and he loves me without words, and it quiets my fears.

"Just like that?" I ask.

"Yes, Amber, I know you. Do you think I didn't notice your board in your bedroom? Or that you never, not once, asked me for anything other than food? Most women would have asked for a car, a house, jewelry, and their child's tuition. And because you didn't, I want to give it all to you and more."

"But what about training camp and the distance?"

"Baby, just let me love you."

"Okay."

EPILOGUE

THE END OF THE SEASON…

WE DIDN'T MAKE it to the playoffs. But I don't care as I exit the plane. I see my boys, but I'm searching for my woman. Amber leans against my Escalade with a smile on her face, and when she steps forward, I stop.

"I think the last man standing just crashed and burned."

"Old Man Kamal, for the record, there is no pact once you two broke it. And mind your damn business." I stop in front of Amber and all jokes leave my brain. "What's going on?"

"Remember when I thought I had food poisoning?"

I chuckle. She's been taking cooking lessons from Kemen and undercooked her chicken. "Yeah, and…?"

"Well, apparently, pulling out is not an effective form of birth control."

"Damn, are we in high school?" Dean chimes in.

"Why did you two come?"

"Because we're your official welcome home crew."

"Get in the truck."

Kamal and Dean leave us alone, and I grab my woman.

"This shouldn't freak you out. But if it does, I understand."

"It doesn't. Now kiss me," I demand pulling her close.

I ran from this, and I snagged a woman and two kids. I back up. "I have a surprise for you too. Get in the truck." I smack her ass and climb in behind the wheel.

On the ride, my thoughts swirl with the truth: I'm having a child. And I feel...happy about it. Maybe it's spending time with Kemen or knowing I'm doing it with Amber, but the thought makes me glad that I set up this surprise for her.

"I hope Miya's done cooking," Amber mumbles.

The Montgomery Compound has been my eyes and ears looking about for Amber and Kemen. And now we're about to make it official.

I stop a few houses before Kamal's house.

"Wrong house. You must be tired."

I jump out and open her door. I hold her hand, and when we reach the front door, I drop the keys in her hand. "It's ours."

Amber stands with her mouth open. She spins around and grabs my face. She kisses me all over and stops with my lips. The depth of her love covers a multitude of pain and hardships. Her love helped me heal and she never asks for perfection. Only honesty and me.

"We can do this any way you want. I just want you beside me."

Her eyes fill with tears, and I know they're the joyful kind. This football season was rough, but I know I'm doing the right thing.

I traveled when I could to keep from disrupting their lives. And once Kemen and Brandon realized they could attend the games in person, we alternated on the weekends the boys didn't have school commitments.

I'm finally talking with Robin. Kemen's killing it in school. I have everyone I love in this city and it's only the beginning.

"Thank you." She kisses me and I know I'm home.

I close the door and lift her skirt. "Ass up, Amber."

Her eyes round. "Do you know what you're doing?"

I strip the clothes off my lady in our new home. Banging comes from the front door and I push deep into her.

"Go home!" Amber yells.

I die laughing. "You're a rare woman, Amber Evans."

"Yeah, I know. I'm a unicorn."

THANK you for reading **GAME OVER**. Emmitt and Amber found their happily-ever after. Please take a few minutes and **leave a review**. I'd love you for life. :)

Coming soon... We have more with the Montgomery family. Who's story should I write next Demetrius or Quan? Email me at info@janesedixon.com and submit your vote.

Be the FIRST to know!

Join My Newsletter
http://www.janesedixon.com/subscribe

Be the first to know about releases and specials. You can unsubscribe anytime.

SNEAK PEEK: PLAY TO WIN

KAMAL & JAYDA'S LOVE STORY

Rules are meant to be broken, and when it comes to love, this ex-quarterback and single mother are playing to win.

Kamal Montgomery owned the football

field, and now he's one-fifth of Southern Soul, a family-owned soul food restaurant. Nothing and no one is off-limits until Jayda enters his restaurant in need of a second chance.

Jayda Dallas returns to Houston with her baby on her hip and her ex in the dust. He refuses to pay child support for their third-year-old daughter, and rather than take his sorry ass back, she's getting a J-O-B.

Jayda stands back, watching women fall at Kamal's feet. His smile is more deadly than his arrogance. But seeing him with her daughter has her wondering if she should take a chance.

Every rejection will only make Kamal's victory sweeter. He plans to lick, taste, and devour her like the delicacy she is until the world, her ex, and Jayda knows his name is tattooed on every inch of her curvy body.

Kamal's never played a game by halves, and Jayda's got a thing or two to show this deviously handsome player. But when an unknown enemy wages war on their budding relationship will their new love survive.

**Get Your Copy on Amazon
or Read in Kindle Unlimited!**

G OLDEN RAYS CUT through the curtains below eye level, casting a faint shadow over my beauty room. Time is passing faster than I can record today. Rocking forward, I flick the blinds a little wider, turning my head to the side, dodging the direct glare of the last hint of the day. I need the light to finish my last video for the week.

The national cosmetic brand paid me five grand to shoot this makeup look for my YouTube channel. The red light signals the camera is recording, and I pick up the fluffy contour brush.

I stare at the camera. "Drugstore makeup can deliver a comparable look to high end makeup if you use the right technique. Watch as I use this foundation as my bronzer." The brush glides over my naturally high cheekbones. The rich brown powder blends with the rose gold highlight.

"Mimicking an 'e' shape will bring the eyes to the center of your beautiful face." I say to my viewers with my eyes on the mirror. Like a trained makeup artist, I dust across my forehead, paying close attention to my temporal bones. My viewers love educational videos and tutorials, throwing in quick tips for help. "And don't forget the little area between the bridge of your nose and your brow bone."

I work quickly because I need to edit this video tonight after Reese goes to sleep. I have this video and four others lined up to publish on my channel while I'm in Houston taking meetings with potential brands with my boyfriend Brett.

In less than five minutes I'm applying my signature natural lip, racing the sun. I reach for my finishing spray.

"Mommy." The door to my beauty room pushes open, not wide enough for me to see in the monitor.

That's my girl. I smile, angling my head to the side, blocking the view from the camera.

"Honey, can Mommy get ten minutes?" Reese peeks around the corner and I hold up both hands, wiggling my fingers, and she nods. "Here, sit with me, they love when you're in my thumbnails." I pat the bench.

She skips through the door with a delightful smile on her face. I can tell she's adding a little extra effort to make her hair fall over her shoulders based on the click-clacking sound of the wooden beads on the end of her braids.

She jumps to an abrupt stop, giggling as the beads slap around. I scoop Reese up and sit her beside me.

"Can I have lip gloss?" She wiggles, getting comfortable while inspecting the makeup and brushes spread out in front of us.

I cut an eye at her. My baby is a genius. I know I'm biased, but she only has to see and hear a thing once to input it into her overactive imagination. It's a task to stay a few steps ahead of her quick wit. She pairs times and sequences with the ease of an older child. At least, I think so, since I had next to no experience with children until I had her. So, we're both learning as we go.

"Yes, but quickly, honey." I kiss the top of her head and rub off the pink residue. Reese yanks open her special drawer in my vanity and digs out her tube of gloss. I smile, watching as she applies it with focus and a steady hand. My nod of approval has my baby beaming as she returns to her drawer for a coloring book. She works on the end of my vanity and I return to finishing my look.

Reese understands makeup is for mommies only. But she also knows I keep special items in the top drawer to keep her occupied while I work. Her favorite item is no doubt her tube of strawberry gloss.

I used to tell her makeup was for big girls only, then we started referring to her as a big girl for going to the potty on her own. My little genius asked within days if she could wear lipstick. I had to think quick, and that's when "we" created Mommy Rules. The first being, lip gloss is for big girls, and makeup is still for mommies.

As a full-time YouTuber, people used to drag me in my comments for letting my daughter wear "makeup." But I block them without a second thought. I draw the line concerning Reese. No if, ands, or buts about it.

What they'll never understand is the power that comes with embracing your beauty. It's not the lipstick or the gloss, but the whisper of confidence that comes with knowing you're the shit, and can't nobody tell you different, even when I find it hard to embrace.

My mother never told me I was beautiful. All I heard was my skin was too dark, my lips were too big, my hips were too wide. I was too much in her eyes. But I can't recall her ever calling me beautiful.

I took to beauty products, hoping to change my appearance with the magic of makeup. Then I worked up the courage to sit in front of the camera.

I started teaching my viewers how to use makeup instead of going under the knife. Pouty lips without fillers. Snatched noses without rhinoplasty. Chiseled cheekbones without surgical sculpting.

It took one video going viral to change my life. More views garnered more attention. More attention brought on more admirers. And I found myself with fans that embrace my ethnic features because I learned to love my wide nose, my full lips, and my striking facial structure.

But in this house, and with Reese, I tell her she's beautiful, inside and out, every single day. Because no one ever told me, except for men interested in my body.

I stop, looking in the mirror. Time to take a few pictures. I face the camera.

"Gems, this is the final look. This is a great base to glam up, or for a beginner playing in makeup. Make the eye more pronounced for a night out with your man or use a bolder lip for drinks with your girls. We're out." I glance down at Reese, who's closing her book, and back to the lens to give my signature sign-off. "And remember Gem, makeup doesn't make you beautiful. You're gorgeous because God made you that way." I wink and give a flirty goodbye wave with my fingers. "Toodles."

"Let me see." Reese stands on the bench with her glossy smile. Her golden skin mirrors her father but her eyes, nose, lips, are all me. "Gorgeous!"

"Thank you, Reesie Piecie. Now let's take this thumbnail." I switch the camera off video to take our picture and pass her the remote. "Ready?"

She nods, hiding the thumb size remote in her little hand. Reese will never doubt her beauty or her worth, and she'll never need a no-good man to tell her she's absolutely perfect.

"Need me to count."

"No, ma'am." Reese stares into the lens like a professional.

"Well, all right then, honey. Let's give them some face."

The camera chimes with the capture of each picture. Reese hits them back to back, giving us time to make slight moves. But we never take our eyes off the camera.

"Silly pose!" Reese squeals. I expand my cheeks like a human blowfish and cross my eyes. "Mommy…" She laughs with a squished face capturing the final picture.

Our laughter echoes through the house. I'm thrilled because we beat the sun. Now that's how to end a night of work. And suddenly the sweetest form of happiness settles over me. To think I never wanted children, but life gave me what I needed, Reese Dallas Hardin—my four-year-old clone.

"How about pizza for dinner?" I close the blinds and turn the camera off.

"And chicken?" Reese drops the remote into my side drawer.

"Yes, I'll order wings too. But you need to take your bath first. Deal?"

"Deal."

"Then chop chop, honey." Reese jumps down and I follow her down the hall with a full face of makeup like I have somewhere to go. But this is my life. Recording videos as an influencer and taking care of my number one priority, Reese. "Get your pjs and I'll start your water."

"Strawberry bubbles, please."

"You got it."

Reese disappears into her bedroom across the hall. It's only seven. I wonder if Brett will make in home in time for dinner. I sit on the edge of the tub pouring in the liquid bubble bath. The sweet fruit fragrance fills the bathroom, and I smile, emptying the basket of her favorite toys into the sudsy water.

"Don't forget your shower cap." I call out, pulling out my cellphone and opening the Message app.

My fingers fly over the screen. *We're ordering pizza and wings. Want your usual?*

I suck in a quick breath, holding my phone. The muscles in my fingers tense from my tight grip. My chest burns from the lack of oxygen, so I exhale until my shoulders buckle. The weight of trying to make our little unit a family is making itself known.

Deep down I know Brett's answer, but that doesn't stop me from hoping that this time I'm wrong. That he'll pick us over his entourage, his boys, and the owner of the pink panties.

"Mommy."

I jump, startled by her standing in the doorway with her nightshirt gathered to her chest. "Yes, baby."

"I need help." I help her out of her clothes and into the tub.

"I'll be right back." I slip out and grab my makeup wipes.

Multitasking is the name of the game in this house. I work around Reese's and Brett's schedules. I'll wash off this makeup and get back to editing the footage after she's in the bed. Before I reach the bathroom, I order the food after checking my messages for Brett's response once more. And true to his nature, there's nothing.

Somehow, we've found ourselves in an awkward "friend zone." It seems no matter how hard I try, or how hard I plead, we're stuck. We live in the same house, share the same bed, yet we live separate lives.

Brett parties all night and sleeps most of the day. I sleep through the night to wake early to care for our child. The moment she's off to school I work to build my relationship with cosmetic and lifestyle brands.

Which went nowhere until Brett connected me with his team. His name wiggled me past the gatekeepers.

Thanks to their efforts I work around the clock. They got me on the public relations list for every major brand. I can barely review all the products I receive, even with recording from sunup to sundown. Hence this trip. His help shifted me from buying products with my money to receiving paid product placements and potentially brand deals. Brett gave me exactly what I wanted but the skeptic in me wonders why, and whether the pink lace panties have anything to do with it.

I turn out the light in Reese's room and hurry down the hall to get my wipes. When I stop at the sink, I chuckle at her splish-splashing in the tub before dropping my phone on the counter and facing my reflection.

For a quick tutorial it turned out well. I lean closer, inspecting my face. Dark brown skin and makeup can be friends or enemies. One brand may cause my rich hue to appear ashy, while another may cause my skin to radiate an inner glow. Overall, I'm pleased. I just hope the footage reflects the flawlessness finish of this soft matte glam look while I'm editing tonight.

Reese strikes up a conversation as I scrub away the layers—powder, foundation, blush, primer—that beautifully cover my imperfections. She flicks water around the bathroom, submerged in her rendition of her play-time fiascos. I don't trip over the small stuff. I'll clean it up after she's in the bed. Instead, I laugh and ask questions, allowing her animated story time to mask the imperfections of my life.

"Tomorrow you're going to Grannie Minnie's. How's that sound? Like fun?"

"Good."

"Yes, ma'am."

I lean over the sink to rinse my face, and I glance up at my bare face. "There you are," I whisper. The doorbell rings and I quickly dry my hands. "That's the food. Finish up, sweetie, so you can eat while it's hot."

I run out the bathroom and down the stairs. Living in a mansion never crossed my mind. My plan was to date for fun and snag a man who could take care of me. The older me laughs at the naivete of my younger self. It was on and popping until the pregnancy test came back positive. And in a flash, I thought my life had ended.

The team sidelined Brett due to an injury, and the pregnancy came at the right time. He had something to focus on other than himself, overlooking the extra pounds I put on and the change in our relationship. I went from a woman he showed off every chance he had, to the mother of his only child.

Ugh. I hate having my identity distilled to my

reproductive organs. Almost more than I hate being his girlfriend for almost five years, or that he and Reese share the same last name. But on the flip side, I can't see forever with Brett.

Not like this. Not since the scales fell from my eyes twenty-three days ago—the moment I found a pair of lace panties in his Bentley. Panties, that don't belong to me. Panties that I would have missed if it wasn't for the circumstances surrounding our trip.

My car was due for a regular service appointment and my list of chores to prepare for staying a week in Houston had me coming and going in circles. So, I needed to drive his car. I stopped by the bank and went fishing in his armrest for a pen, and there I found them. Hot pink lace, folded, tucked away, damn near neon against the charcoal black interior.

I should be pissed. Right?

Throwing shit.

Cussing his ass out.

Reminding him I gave birth to his child. Flaunting every stretch mark, my less than perky breasts, and my fuller hips. Reminding him of how he begged me to have Reese, to move into his house, and to make our situationship a family.

How can a slither of lace untangle the fabric of the life I'm desperately trying to hold together? I stop by the table in the front hallway and grab some cash for the tip from the drawer.

I guess... I stall for a moment, attempting to make sense of the unreasonable. But I guess I'm not pissed, because I'm not shocked. The panties, oddly, confirmed what I already knew. Brett and I haven't had sex in months. It's been so long I refuse to put a date to it, and if he's not getting it from me, he's getting it from someone.

I know.

I was that girl.

The girl who didn't care about a man's responsibilities at home as long as he kept me clothed in designer labels and rocking the most expensive handbags. But somewhere between giving birth to our daughter and finding those cheap-ass-lace-hot-pink panties, I realize I've changed.

Apparently, it took me four years to grow the fuck up and now the overwhelming question is... What do I plan to do about it?

I plaster a smile on my face and open the wooden door. The delivery guy and I make small talk as he stacks scorching hot boxes in my arms. I bid him goodbye and hustle to the kitchen, placing them on the island.

Because the old Jayda Dallas would have told his ass to kick rocks. But the new Jayda knows it's not about me anymore. This is my baby's life too. So, instead of wilding the fuck out, like I wanted to do… like I want to… I swallowed my frustration with this relationship, my discontentment with my lack of autonomy, and I had a come to Jesus moment.

I prayed.

Prayed hard. So hard the sky parted and rained. I figure the Man upstairs had a good laugh at my expense.

Me, who had no regard for others. Me, who strongly considered whether to keep my child. Me, who has absolutely nothing to offer the world except my pretty face and makeup skills.

I spread the boxes out like a makeshift buffet, placing the roll of paper towels at one end and the pitcher of juice on the other. Then I pull down two plates, one for her and one for me.

Funny thing is, I didn't know when the shift began. Those panties make it hard to pretend I'm happy. That our relationship is the same. But what other choice do I have?

I cook and clean like normal. I record videos and smile for the camera. However, deep in my soul, I wonder if this is payback for the hell I've caused. I went from an independent woman to a woman with a child, living in his house, driving his cars. So, I brushed it under the carpet.

Then a few weeks ago, Milton, the new brand manager, invited us to Houston to meet with a few luxury boutiques. I jumped at the chance to fly back to Texas. Houston isn't home, but my best friend, Catrina, lives there. My hope, I guess, best case is Brett and I can rekindle our relationship. Worst case, Catrina and I can down a bottle of wine and help me get my shit together.

"Mommy."

"Coming and don't stand in the tub, I'm on my way." I take the stairs two at a time, stopping by the hall closet for a towel. I push the door open, and my heart drops. The sight of my child stops me dead in my tracks.

"Reese, how did you get bubbles in your hair?" I fight to hold back my laughter. We spent hours braiding her hair.

"I'm a princess."

"With a bubble crown?"

"Yes, ma'am."

I squat beside the tub, cupping her face in my hands and kiss the tip of her nose. "Baby, the point of the shower cap is to not get your hair wet."

"Sorry, Mommy."

I help her up and wrap my strawberry-scented child in the fluffy towel. I made this bed and I wouldn't change anything if it means I'd have her. So, if it means stuffing my desires to give her a chance in life, with a mother and father raising her, I'll do it. She's worth it.

Ten minutes later, we're in the kitchen talking with our mouths full, when the hum of the garage door opening silences us. And I swear my baby shrinks in her skin. The sight wraps around my heart and squeezes me so tight I can't breathe. Then a car door slams.

"Eat, baby. It's getting late." I stand and kiss her forehead, not missing her slight tremble. Her stares at the door behind me. I turn her face to mine. "Want some juice?"

She nods, and I miss the light in her eyes. The mother in me wants to give her anything and every-thing that will make her happy. That's why I overlook the changes I see in Brett.

The late nights. The whispering phone calls. The broken promises. The side door opens, and he's startled straight.

"I'll talk to you tomorrow," Brett mumbles, ending his phone call, stumbling a little. "Hey… my girls."

"Did you drive yourself home?" The stench of alcohol drowns out the smell of pepperoni. I stand beside Reese and she leans into me—by instinct I hold her. Brett stands taller, he towers over my five-and-a-half-foot frame, as his smokey eyes bounce between Reese and my protective arm around her shoulder.

"No, I came through the garage to keep from

digging out my keys. What are you guys doing up?" He smiles down at Reese, dropping the device into his pocket.

"We're finishing up dinner. I'll make you a plate."

"Nah, I'm good, I ate with…" He stops himself.

The room falls deathly silent. I play the mediator between Brett and Reese. He regards her like an expensive possession, bragging about her and sharing her photos on social media. I know he loves her, but he's more like a friend than a father.

Which makes all my sacrifices seem futile. We stay because I want my daughter raised in a two-parent household. I want Reese to have a relationship with her father. Both are things I never had, and Reese deserves that and more.

"Okay… Then join us. Are you packed for the trip?" I sit and pull Reese's plate closer to her. "Milton sent over the itinerary for the week. We have a jam-packed schedule, but it should be fun."

"I need to lie down. Goodnight." Brett walks past us.

I glare at his retreating back. I have a choice here. Follow him or let it slide. Again. Then I look down at the tears gathered in my baby's eyes. The man's using her heart like a cheap trampoline.

"Daddy's just tired." She nods beneath my chin, as if she understands. But no child should understand his asshole ways. I want to follow him, but Reese comes first. "Finish your pizza and I have a special treat for you."

She sits back and smiles. "Cookies?"

"I don't know… maybe."

I squeeze her tight and give her a shake to make her giggle and her beads clang like windchimes. I walk over to the refrigerator and grab her a juice box. Then I do what I do best, change the subject.

"Want to stop and get some new coloring books?" I take a bite of my pizza, showing my baby how to brush it off. I'll have all night to process what just happened. But for now we'll focused on the next positive thing on her list and that's spending the next with Grandma Minnie, Brett's mother. She truly makes up for where her son falls short.

"One of those big ones like last time?" She loves the huge floor-sized coloring books.

"We'll stop by the store in the morning."

We finish dinner and clean the kitchen together. I get her to bed, and she's sleep within minutes. I exhale, mentally preparing myself for the second half of my day. It's time to edit, upload, and schedule all the videos I recorded today. I drag to my feet and flick on the soft purple nightlight, then I slip out, leaving her door cracked.

Reese sleeps like a rock. Once she's out, she's out. I

chuckle, heading down the hall to my beauty room, and I surprised by the sound of Brett talking on the phone.

I glance at my watch—it's after midnight. He jumps a little when I yank the door open. "Would it have hurt you to sit and talk with her tonight? She missed seeing you all day."

"Don't start, Jayda. I'm exhausted."

"Not too tired to whisper on the phone." I gesture to his ever-present device.

A part of me wants to get it and see the evidence of all of his dirty deeds. But my pride won't let me do it. I promised myself the moment I turn into that woman, it's over. It's a shaky line, but it's all I got.

"Man, whatever." He rolls over in the bed, as if I'm not standing here. Then he glances back over his shoulder, "And since you're already bitchin', I'm not going to Houston."

"What? Then I'll stay home too." The words spill out, but this is a big break for me. For once, I'm carving out my own space and my own career, but it's not more important than my family.

"No, go. This trip is important. If you sign with these boutiques, more will follow."

"If it's so important, why are you staying here?"

"I'm meeting with a new potential client."

"A client?"

"Seems the word is spreading. I received an inquiry from another beauty blogger."

I can't see his face, but I hear the sarcasm in his tone. Brett was playing pro football when we met. Then he injured himself. After riding the bench, they let him go. Now, the very thing he used to laugh at is how I generate additional income.

He thought my YouTube channel was a joke until Milton approached me, and then Brett gave himself the title of my manager.

I had the followers and fans, but now I'm a brand with the verified blue checks and all.

"They'll expect to see my manager at these meetings," I remind him.

"Milton will fly out in two days. You can handle things for a few days?"

"I've handled things for years. So, you'll look after Reese? This would be a great time for you two to bond and..."

"No, my mom is looking forward to spending the week with her." He leans back against the headboard, staring at his phone.

I cross my arms. This picture is much clearer to me. His doggish ways know no boundaries. "And this will leave you plenty of time to do what you do."

"Quit tripping." He smiles, licking his lips before

he completes the text message. Then he drops his phone onto the nightstand.

I stand in the dark, staring at his silhouette. All I can think about are those pink panties and the fact that I'm scheduled to remain in Houston for an entire week, and Brett will be here alone. He flips around a few times before settling, not bothering to look my way, or tell me goodnight.

Visions of panties and bras lingering over my house bombard my mind. He wouldn't... *Would he?*

Brett would. He'll have some skank in our bed before I can leave Reese at Minnie's house. And like a fool, I'm still with him. Still trying to make this dysfunctional unit a family.

I turn my head up to the ceiling, ready to plead with the Man above again. But why should He listen? I got exactly what I wanted: A man to match my swag. A man that is financially secure. A man every woman wants. A man that makes heads turn.

A man not ready to settle down, whispered through my head. And the old Jayda breaks through the haze of my uncertainty with a healthy dose of taught love.

Jayda, now might be the right time to wake the fuck up!

CHAPTER 2

"Smell that?" I rolled down my window and let the aroma of my mother's fried chicken fill the rented car. If it's possible for a scent to invoke the feeling of being home, it's my mother's food.

My mouth waters, signaled by the gurgle of my stomach, and for a brief second I hate I agreed to let Trish accompany me. We're stopping on the way to Los Angeles for a gathering with mutual friends. I suggested she visit the mall or check into the hotel without me, but she insisted on joining me for brunch.

My fingers wrap around the chrome handle and a wave of excitement ripples through me. My younger brothers—Rashaad, Demetrius, and Quan—and our baby sister Miya save a table inside since it's crowded. I don't know which excites me more, seeing them or eating at Southern Soul.

I haven't visited home for more than a quick pop-in here and there since our folks remarried five years ago. And I haven't had my mother's chicken and waffles, or shrimp and grits, or.... "Come on, let's get going."

"You're taking me here?" Her wrinkled nose and displeased gaze say she's the fancy type.

I shake my head. Why didn't I leave her in New York? That's my bad for bringing her. Emmitt, my boy since college, introduced us, and I should have known something was up when he introduced us, instead of dating her himself.

I turn back to the old building, the unpaved parking lot, and the tasty cloud lingering out back over the smoker. The line wraps across the front sidewalk and down the side, which I'd expect on a Saturday.

"Yeah, got a problem with it?"

"I guess not, but I expected…" Her eyes swept the area until her doe-like expression returns to mine. Then she hesitates, "It's fine."

I need to tell my boy Emmitt, Trish isn't my type. I like a woman that can hang in the hood, on the ski slopes, or at the governor's mansion, in the same day. My life covers it all, and any woman on my arm must adapt.

Timberlands. Stilettos. Flip-flops. I want it all, and stuck-up Trish may not make the cut.

I open the door, placing my feet on the land I

know like I know the football field, like I know my own face because this place is home for me. I round the car, opening the door for Trish. We'll eat and head to do some shopping before flying out to Los Angeles.

I extend an arm to her, glancing into her eyes. This place is in the Fifth Ward in Houston. For most, it's the hood, but this is my old stomping grounds. Her heels crunch on the gravel as we approached the line. The old building seems smaller, a little more weather worn, and in need of a coat of paint.

"Yo, man, is that you, Kamal? What'd up with you?" A big man with a linebacker's build steps closer.

"Man, I can't call it. How's your family? And your folks?" Recognition settles the moment I hear Rodrick's laugh. We played ball in junior high and high school. We pound fists.

"Good. Good. Just trying to get in here and break bread with my ole lady. Can we get a picture with you? Been telling my lady I taught you everything you know on the field." His arm circles the woman beside him and pulls her forward.

"Taught me everything I know, huh? Still a bullshitter, I see." I smile, he's always had a large personality.

"Oh, then you know Rodrick well." The woman grins.

"Shut up Yvonne and take a picture with the man."

We share a laugh as the two bicker a little. I unfold Trish's hand from my arm and the two flank me.

I take Rodrick's phone and snap the picture, giving it back to him. "Don't forget to tag me."

"No doubt, man. Thanks. Wish the kids were here."

"Bring them by sometime. My number's still the same. I hop in and out of town."

"Word?" His eyebrows shoot up, as if surprised.

"I don't let this shit go to my head. We're still peoples. Now don't abuse it. But I'd love to meet your kids."

"Man, you were always my boy." He beams, stepping back in line.

"What are you up to now?"

He digs out a card and passes it over to me. "I have a private security company. We handle events, private detail, you name it I have a guy for your needs."

"I'll remember that." I slip the card in my pocket. "Look, I gotta run. Enjoy your meal and thanks for the support."

We make our way to the doors. A few more people stop me while others frown. I stop at the podium, smiling at the hostess.

"Good morning, Catrina." Her lips curl into a welcoming smile and I return it. I pull out my phone to call my brother while I scan the crowd.

"They're waiting for you over there." Catrina points to the dining room facing the street.

"Wait, this is a group date?" Trish halts, causing us both to stop.

"I told you I'm here to check on my family. You still wanted to accompany me." I hold up a finger to my brother, Rashaad, and face Trish. I glance at my watch and drop my hands in my pockets. This "date" started five hours ago. She talked the entire ride over, name dropping to show me she's part of the "in crowd" in NYC. Now, I'm ready to eat and kick it with my sibling. I glance over and seeing all of them at the table makes me eager to find a solution with Trish.

"How about I call you a ride back to the hotel?" Then I sweeten the offer. "I can make us reservations and we can hit up a few spots around town later tonight."

The sour look glued to her face since we parked disappears. "That sounds more like it."

I pull out my phone to call a car service.

"No need, I got it." She tips her head to the waiting car. "You have my number, call me when you're ready." She sashays off without a glance back.

I shake my head and chuckle. I'm not surprised. She's here to be seen and not at a hole in the wall restaurant. Southern Soul is about rolling up your sleeves and devouring Southern comfort foods. There's nothing glamorous about it, just good food in a family environment.

"Yo, Big Boy, the biscuits are getting cold," Q calls out over my shoulder.

"Don't start that Big Boy shit with me." I stroll over to the table. My brothers and sister stand to greet me. We collide in a familiar huddle, then I give each my undivided attention.

"What the superstar is too good for his nickname?" Q and I execute our signature handshake, ending with a salute. Then I gather his big ass in my arms. "Man, stop!"

The others laugh while I rough him up. Quan was the baby for years until our folks surprised us with their *oops* baby, and the only Montgomery dressed in pink, Miya. I turn and face my baby that's not a baby but a grown woman.

"Baby Miya." Her arms circle my waist and I hold her tight. "I missed you, love."

Miya glances up with a smile. "Not enough to bring your player ass home. Who was that?"

"Nobody. Trying to multitask. So, what's the emergency that required flying home?" She steps back, making room for Demetrius, the middle child always quietly observing the world. "How's the book coming along?"

"Slow, but I'm not in a rush. What about you? Are

you planning to stick around for more than the week-end?" Demetrius grounds me with a firm hand on the shoulder.

The thought of staying in the city more than a weekend means I'm bound to bump into Kenneth, and I'm not there yet.

"And your niece needs more than weekly FaceTime calls." Rashaad adds, stopping behind his chair.

Their expectant faces make me feel trapped yet grounded. Each standing behind a chair awaiting my response. Man, I miss my family.

I never thought I'd settled anywhere but Houston, but our parents remarrying changed everything. The fourth largest city in the United States isn't big enough for Kenneth and I to live.

"I'll see what I can do and tell my girl I'll be by to get her for a day of the works."

"She'll be packed and ready to go. Now let's eat." Rashaad laughs, taking the attention off me and back to food.

My chair is at the head of the table. I sit scanning the table and pride fills my chest—like a proud father. Each of my siblings are thriving and it shows. As the eldest of the five Montgomery children, I raised them like my own from the moment our mother signed the divorce papers. At thirteen I became the man of the house and I took my role seriously.

None of my siblings have seen the inside of a jail cell, although Q had a few close calls. None of them were teenage statistics. All of them are college educated and successful in their chosen fields.

"What's so important that y'all couldn't share it over the phone?" The collective shift of the energy sends a chill down my spine. "What is it? Is it Mother?" I guess since she's not here.

"You could say that." Rashaad flags down the waitress. "We're ready for our orders."

"Well, don't all speak at once."

A series of unspoken messages bounce between them until the ball drops in Rashaad's lap. He's the second oldest and the one that keeps me in the loop. My decision to live on the east coast following my retirement from the league put a wedge between us, and that's something I need to repair.

"The folks are ready to retire." Rashaad shrugs, leaning back with an arm resting against the table. The casual posture speaks volumes.

"And?" I grab a buttermilk biscuit from the basket and my stomach stirs.

"*And*... they want us to take over the restaurants." Miya bookends the announcement.

"It shouldn't surprise us. I just wasn't expecting it this soon." I glance around the room, seeing Southern Soul with fresh eyes. We were raised in this building.

The school bus picked us up and dropped us off at the end of that gravel driveway.

The place once served cafeteria style, then we added waiters before I left for college. Then I had the place expanded when I landed a contract as a professional football player. We added windows to bring in more natural light and updated the restrooms and kitchen. But that was almost fifteen years ago.

"Kamal…" Q interrupts my musing. "This place isn't what it used to be."

"What do you mean? It's packed. There's isn't an empty seat in the dining room, and there's still a line outside."

"On Saturdays, but Monday through Friday it's a ghost town. Mom's not making enough to support the staff, let alone moving—"

"Moving?"

They share a grimace.

"They're ready to turn over the reins and sell the house too." Q says, the fidgety tap of his fingers captures my attention more than his words.

"Sell the house?" I turn to Rashaad. "Is it listed?"

"Not yet, but Mom's already consulted a stager and started removing our things."

"And what does *Kenneth* have to say about all of this?" I toss the biscuit back in the basket. "I'm sure this is all his idea. Probably filling her head with more of his fucking lies."

"Dad says it's her idea," Miya says.

"Yeah, right? To give up her home, her business, leave her children and grandchild behind. Sounds like more of his manipulation to me." I pinch the bridge of my nose. "It was only a matter of time. He wants to get her away from us. And then what?"

I want to stand up and walk the length of the room, but that's not possible. The last time I attempted to talk with Mother about her rekindled a relationship with our father, it was on their wedding day. She shut me down and told me it wasn't any of my business. I honored her wish to walk her down the aisle, but our relationship changed.

Now Kenneth and I respect each other's boundaries, and my mother's wishes. And our "conversations" are nothing more than common pleasantries, since he walked out on us twenty years ago.

"I think he's on the up and up," Q says.

"And you, Demetrius?" I glance over at him, sitting on the other side of Miya.

"He seems different. But I don't trust him."

"Rashaad?"

"I don't want to think the worse, but Mom's house is worth at least two million dollars. Two point five if we list at the right time."

I whistle, not realizing the house had appreciated in value over the years. But with the renovations we did for her birthday a few years back and the new construction in her subdivision, I'm not surprised. She owns a house inside the loop. People would pay a pretty penny to get their hands on that property, even if only to level the house and build something larger.

"So, you think he's trying to get in her purse?" My heart races like the moment a play is called on the field, as I contemplate my next move.

"Man, I don't know. But she always said she'd never leave Houston. Especially with me having Lillian." Rashaad has full custody of his six-year-old daughter after his nasty divorce last year.

"Miya?" I ask.

"I think he's changed. He's not the same man he was when we were kids." Her compassionate eyes plead with each of us, but Miya's always been a daddy's girl. "I think we should give him a chance. People change."

"When people show you their true colors, you paint that shit in ink." I chuckle, but nothing about this predicament is funny. I don't trust the man. He left us once, and I don't put it past him to do again. "The moment I believe Kenneth is different is the moment y'all can commit my ass to the crazy house. Have y'all talked with Mother, alone? And why is this the first time I'm hearing about this?"

"Mom's an adult. I make it a point to stay out of her personal affairs." Rashaad lifts a hand in the air in resignation. "I figured she'd tell you when she's ready. As for this meeting, we called you in because of our growing concern for the restaurant."

I glance around at the business in question, not pleased with being left in the dark about this matter. I open my mouth to respond and see the waitress approaching the table.

I sit back to give her room. She places the plates of food on the table while I mull over the news. Our parents were joint owners. During their divorce they agreed to split the business in half, while keeping the Southern Soul name intact.

Southern Soul Houston went to Mother, and Southern Soul Raleigh went to Kenneth. I haven't visited the Raleigh location since my early teens, and the effect of their remarriage on the business never crossed my mind. Not when the business documentation has us listed as equal owners. Therefore, any significant changes would need the majority approval of each of us. That fact gives me some relief, but our contracts mean nothing if Kenneth is playing with my mother's heart.

A plate blocks my vision for a moment. The corners of my lips turn up as the scent of my mother's signature spices tickles my nose. The oversized waffle covers the plate topped with four perfectly fried chicken wings. Miya squeezes my hand, and I know she ordered.

"You're a real one," I tell her and grab my fork.

"You know it." Miya winks, slipping the utensil from my hand, and intertwines our fingers.

I almost forgot. I sit straight up and scan their faces, waiting for me. "Demetrius, will you bless the food?"

"Father…"

All heads bow. His words float in and out of my mind. He prays over the food, our family, over the decisions we must make. We end with a boisterous "amen." I linger for a moment, looking over my siblings.

"Rome wasn't built in a day, brother," Q calls out, smothering his scrambled eggs in salsa.

I nod and pick up my fork. I guess I need to shift my schedule and head over to Mother's to get to the bottom of this change. What I know without a doubt is Kenneth won't get his hands on Southern Soul Houston.

"Eat before it gets cold. You know how you hate cold chicken." Miya passes the hot maple syrup.

"Yes, ma'am." I take her offer and cover the piping hot food with a thick coating. I'll eat now and handle this situation later. I cut into the waffles, eager for nostalgia to settle in as the sweet batter melts on my tongue.

The food lightens the mood as we shift from family

business to catching up on life. Lillian in elementary school. Rashaad expanding his real estate agency. Miya considering whether to move back home for good.

"I'm glad you finally dumped that jerk."

"I'm starting to think all men are jerks." Miya picks at her food.

"Damn, throw us all under the bus with his loser ass. We told you he was a player," Q says.

"Q, you belong under that damn bus. All of y'all, except Rashaad. Lining up women like trophies. One day, you'll find you match."

"Like you found yours," he teases. Q isn't one to hold his tongue and the two of them stay at each other's throats.

"Q, keep playing with me." She thrusts a fork in his direction.

"What are you going to do now?" I ask Miya.

"Look for a job here. I want to find a place I can stretch my creativity. Maybe become a head chef."

"I have a few connections in the city," I offer.

"Not now, I plan to take some time off. Hit the gym. Focus on myself for a change."

I exchange looks with Demetrius. I caught that "hit the gym" and he did too.

"Miya, there's nothing men like more than a sexy, confident curvy woman." I have two true loves and she's one of them. Knowing some no-good man has her doubting herself makes me want to find him and express my displeasure.

"Correction. Purchased curves. Not real ones."

"Baby Miya's on a roll." Q smiles, trying to get under her skin.

I wish I could reach him. Then I look at the next best thing. "Rashaad…"

Like a mind reader, Rashaad pops the back of Q's head and our laughter fills the room.

"Don't kill the messenger," Q barks, sliding away from Rashaad.

I wipe at my tears as he rubs the back of his head. That's when I see a beauty outside the bay window.

She steps out of a silver luxury car. Her brown skin so rich it looks photoshopped. The fitted business suit contours her curvy frame, stopping midthigh.

Sexy…

She spins around to gather her luggage, when her head tips back and I assume she's laughing at the driver. Her hair floats around her oval face and I smile, as if hearing it. Then she takes the offered business card, giving the driver a sultry smile, and my breath catches.

I lean forward, unable to look away as the driver stumbles a little, spellbound. I don't blame the brother. I freeze, watching the scene unfold until the driver pulls away. Then she turns, heading this way.

"Excuse me." I drop my napkin beside my plate and

head out to meet the black beauty. She's rolling Louis Vuitton luggage over gravel like it's smooth concrete.

"This ninja is always recruiting," Q says behind me, but I'm focused on the door.

I stroll through the crowd and out the door. She turns, mumbling at the luggage, lowering until she tilts her curvy backside in the air.

I see you, baby… I don't stop until I'm beside her. "Let me help you with that."

∽

Continue Reading…

**Get Your Copy on Amazon
or Read in Kindle Unlimited!**

KEEP YOUR KINDLE BLAZIN'

Blazin' Love (Contemporary Romance)

Complete Series

Platinum Love (Book 1)

Privileged Love (Book 2)

Exclusive Love (Book 3)

Chosen Love (Book 4)

Special Love (Book 5)

Absolute Love (Book 6)

Pretend for Me (A Short Story)

Devoted Love (Book 7)

Select Love (Book 8)

Lavish Love (Book 9)

Total Love (Book 10)

Forbidden Chords Series (Contemporary Romance)

Complete Series

Hidden Desire (Prequel)

Rockstar Seduction (Prequel)

Rockstar Secrets (Book 1)

Rockstar Sinners (Book 2)

Rockstar Savages (Book 3)

Waiting for You (A Short Story)

This Song's for You (A Short Story)

Rockstar Scandals (Book 4)

Precious Stones Series (Romantic Suspense)

Before Black Diamond (Prequel)

Black Diamond (Book 1)

African Emerald (Book 2)

Fire Opal (Book 3)

Southern Gentlemen (Slow Burn Steamy Romance)

Play to Win (Book 1)

All Yours (Book 2)

Honest and True (Book 3)

Game Over (Book 4)

Smith Pact Duo (Contemporary Romance)

Complete Series

Yuki's Luck (Book 1)

Tempting Asher (Book 2)

Smith Surprise (Book 3)

When It Comes to Love Boxed Set (Books 1 - 3)

Weekend Reads

Resort to Love

You Owe Me

Grown and Sexy for Christmas

Serial Fiction

Secret Desires

See all of my books on my website:

http://www.janesedixon.com/books.

ABOUT THE AUTHOR

USA Today Bestseller, Ja'Nese Dixon writes tales of romance laced with strong women, stronger men, and family values that based on more than blood. Her happily ever afters are written to inspire. So, if you're looking for a page turner that will leave you blushing, with your heart racing, and lying to yourself about reading "just one more chapter" then grab one of the author's thirty-something books.

Ja'Nese is an avid reader and coffee drinker living in Houston, TX with her husband, three adult children, and her spoiled diva dog. Want to learn more? Join her newsletter and get exclusive reads, all the inside details, and a first look at what's to come at www.-janesedixon.com.

Stay in Touch:
www.janesedixon.com
info@janesedixon.com

facebook.com/AuthorJaNeseDixon

twitter.com/janesedixon

instagram.com/authorjanesedixon

amazon.com/author/janesedixon

bookbub.com/authors/ja-nese-dixon

ABOUT THE PUBLISHER

Purpose Prevails Publishing
2231B Center St. STE 144
Deer Park, TX 77536
www.purposeprevailspublishing.com

Get Waiting for You for FREE!

Do you love second chance romances? Then here's another sweet, steamy romance for your device.

https://geni.us/waitingforyougift

63048921R00176